TAKEN
BY THE
DARK ELF
KING

CHARLOTTE SWAN

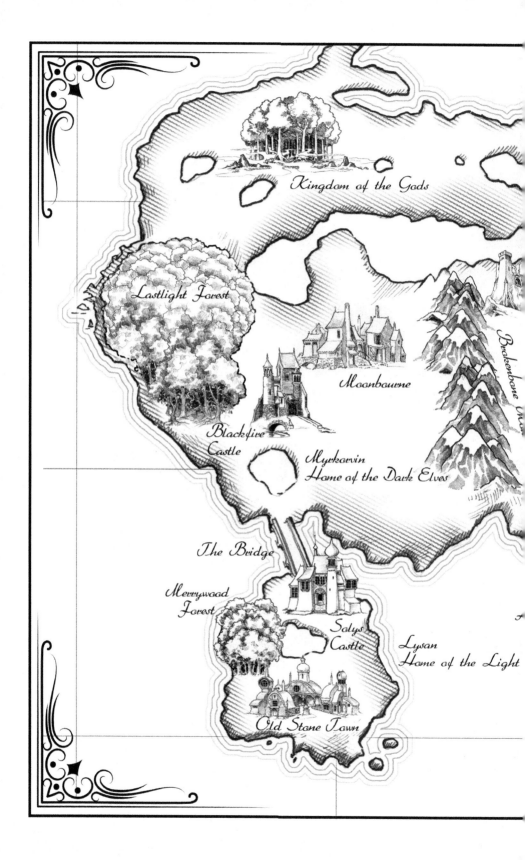

eBook ISBN: 979-8-9870192-0-7
Paperback ISBN: 979-8-9870192-1-4

Cover Art by Magdalena Pietrzak (@barnswallow.art)
Cover Design by Haya Designs
Map & Interior Formatting by Qamber Designs & Media
Editing by Aquila Editing

www.authorcharlotteswan.com

For my mom and dad. I hope you never, ever read this…

CONTENT/TRIGGER WARNINGS & TROPES

CW/TW: Death of a Parent(s), Misogyny, Violence/Gore, Kidnapping, Dub-Con, FMC Threatened to be SA'd (not by MMC)

Tropes: Breeding Kink, 'Touch Her and I'll Kill You', Arranged Marriage, Scarred Hero, Fated Mates, Praise Kink

CHAPTER ONE

ELVIE

I T IS NEVER A GOOD thing when the castle is quiet.

The last time the throne room was this silent was when Lord Elowyn had been found guilty of abusing his tenants. He had treated the farmers inside of his domain as chattel, useful only for working the land to line his pockets with more gold. How many humans had dropped dead before word had spread to my father? Hundreds by some estimates.

My father, the king, had Elowyn's legs broken and tossed him on a boat to the Shadowkeep Bay, home to countless bloodthirsty pirates.

Elowyn's son rules now, and he is of a much milder nature. He's hopeful the fate that befell his father never lands on him. As light elves, we may view ourselves as the more civilized of the two, but we are not spotless. Our soft faces just hide what we really are.

Unlike the hulking figure that stands in the middle of the throne room now. There is no hiding what he is. The height. The snow-white hair and skin the color of soot. Eyes that glow red with a burning fire. He is a dark elf. Our monstrous brethren from the north. A royal guard from the King of Myrkorvin himself.

You would think a wild beast had found its way into the palace. Servants rushing from rooms, heads bowed low, moving on silent feet. Mothers and nannies keeping their children close to their side. Still holding on to those old tales that dark elves snatch children to feed to the horned beasts they keep under Blackfire Castle.

There is no truth to those tales, my nanny once told me; but looking at this figure standing in front of us, it is hard to not believe it.

1

As the only princess of Lysan, my place is to stand on the left side of my mother when we receive important guests. My brothers mirror my position on the opposite side of my father. My brother Garren is scowling so intensely I fear his eyes may pop from his skull. A most embarrassing event to occur in front of our guest.

My other brother, Briar, looks as if he cannot be bothered. He regards our visitor with as much interest as he paid our royal tutors. Disdain and boredom written all over his face. Like this is more of an inconvenience than an act of diplomacy.

Me? Well, I am not quite sure how I look standing up here. My gown is the color of Lysan gold; it mirrors my mother's. Rich as the first rays of morning sun, glimmering in the light filtering in from the glass ceiling above us. Perhaps I look discontented, as I have not mastered my mother's perfect look of severe serenity.

My mother tells me I have storm clouds in my eyes. A reflection of the curiosity brewing in my mind, wanting to find any means of escape. When I was younger, I wanted nothing more than to have her warm golden eyes. Now, at twenty-three, I am well past my first blood and have fully settled into my elven form. Silver eyes and all.

Perhaps our visitor sees the curiosity on my face as his ruby gaze rakes over me and turns to my parents.

"Your Majesties," the visitor says in a voice as cold as steel.

My father is staring down at him. Even though the king's throne is perched on a dais, the dark elf in front of us does not even need to raise his chin to make eye contact with my father. My parents sit on the throne of Lysan, a massive golden tree trunk with two seats forged into it. The second seat was added the day my father met my mother, knowing her to be his queen the instant he saw her. And there she has sat ruling beside him for the last five and a half centuries.

Before the war, visits from Myrkorvin were commonplace. The old dark elf king did not let his people live as secluded as their new king has. Garren says that after the Orc Wars, their new king used the death of his parents to consolidate power. Removing the light elves from their ancestral lands as punishment for not assisting enough during the war.

2

My brother was there the day the old king fell. He watched as the new king rose from the blood and decimated the Orc hordes in one evening of carnage. The dark elves had always been animals, but this new king was nothing short of a demon.

"To what do we owe this visit from Myrkorvin? We trust that your king is in good health," my father replies evenly.

"Our king is very well; he is the reason for my visiting you here today, Your Grace." The visitor digs into the satchel at his waist, the black of his armor looking like spilled ink in the morning sun. He hands an envelope to one of my father's guards, a blood-red seal stamped on the front, and my father regards it carefully before snapping the wax.

His eyes scan the parchment and then widen, his head snapping up.

"A ball? The king wishes to throw a *ball*? After years of separation he is allowing our people to reunite for a night of…dancing?" My father is in disbelief. To be fair, he is not the only one. Garren's face remains twisted in disgust. A few of the lords and ladies in attendance cover their mouths with gloved hands. As my eyes continue to scan the crowd, they land on a figure in the back.

Lucien's pale green eyes light when ours connect. He is handsome, tall and lean as most of our elven males are. A crop of dark hair that was soft when I had held it in my hand. Unfortunately, that had been the only aspect of our coupling that deserved praise. He had been too eager, too clumsy, too *excited* to be lying with the princess of Lysan.

A word to males, the last thing a female wants to be reminded of when they are fucking is their noble and long-lasting lineage.

I quickly avert my eyes from his. Lucien had been in the right place during the summer's harvest last month where I had partaken in a few too many glasses of berry wine. A mistake that I will be diligent never to make again. Elven males are too capricious. Human men at least feel grateful just for the chance to touch an elf.

I smile at the memory of my first human lover. A beautiful boy who had come to us as an apprentice in our royal stables. He had been so in awe of our kind and even though we had been the same sixteen years, there was always a maturity to him. Better to bed him than some four hundred-year-old male claiming me on my wedding day, producing the bloody sheets in an archaic tradition, signifying his male veracity.

Most of our kind had parted ways with those values but some still held firm to them.

"Not just for dancing. King Arkain is opening his gate to you and your people so that they may have the chance to participate in The Night of a Hundred Faces. Surely, you remember when that was a common Myrkorvin tradition, King Orvian?"

My mother shakes her head, answering instead. "The last time one of those was held was when I was a girl over five centuries ago. The old king was mated to his queen. His son, we were under the impression, was resigned to finding his mate as well. We assumed this tradition was lost to time. Or that the king was simply to live without a bride."

There is unease in her tone. The Night of a Hundred Faces? I've never heard of this before. It is certainly not a tradition we have in Lysan.

"Our king has been advised that he has lived in solitude for too long. And in that spirit, he too believes our two people have been separated long enough—"

"And whose fault is that? Not ours," Garren grounds out. My father cuts him a sharp, silencing look.

"Yes," the visitor continues, "the War and those infernal Orcs who claimed the lives of our king's beloved parents blinded him. He knows now that it was grief and loss that caused him to be so harsh. He wishes to use this night as the first step in repairing bonds between our two kingdoms."

"Seems like a trick. As is common for your kind," my brother sneers. "How can we trust that once we are over the bridge the *king* does not have assassins waiting for us."

"We know you are wary of our kind. That we have always been at odds with each other but should the Orcs rise again it will take all of us to defeat them." The visitor pauses. "Besides, this land holds no great appeal for our kind. Killing you would create a hostile people, keeping the throne would be near impossible for our king."

Garren opens his mouth to argue further but my father holds up a hand.

"Does King Arkain believe the Orcs are mounting an offensive?"

The visitor inclines his head, that red stare seeming to glow brighter.

"At this point we do not know, but the king would rather have us on our way to a united front than wait until it is too late to act." The visitor removes his helmet. There are audible gasps at the sight he makes. Gruesome in this unforgiving light, there are claw marks marring the left side of his face. Raised and puckered white skin, stark against his ashy gray complexion.

"You were there, King Orvian, when the Orcs first attacked. Your son was there when the old king fell, when his widowed queen perished in grief right alongside him. I was there for every battle. If the Orcs rise again, they will not stop at Myrkorvin, and without us there to help you, Lysan will fall to them."

"We could destroy the bridge," Garren counters.

The visitor turns his disfigured face towards my brother's smooth one. How two males could have lived through the same event, one scared forever and one untouched, seemed like an unjust contrast. With a smirk curving his dark gray lips, white teeth with fangs sharper than our own, the visitor shakes his head.

"Orcs are marvelous swimmers, Prince."

My brother's face turns a deep shade of purple, his hand grasping for the sword at his waist. Ridiculous. Like a child throwing a temper tantrum. My brother and I do not often see eye to eye. My mother likes to remind me that out of all her children he was the calmest baby. Now? That temper is going to be what gets him killed one day.

"It says here that the ball is in two weeks time?" my father asks.

The visitor turns his gaze away from my brother and stows his helmet.

"Yes, Your Majesty. Royal escorts will be posted on both sides of the bridge. The king is offering safe passage to anyone who wishes to attend the festivities." The visitor turns to look at the surrounding room of nobles. "Blackfire Castle and its surrounding grounds will be warded to protect against any beasts who may come sniffing. The king guarantees your safety for the entirety of the event."

The visitor bows his head and my father nods.

"Tell your king that my family and I will attend." Garren lets out a strangled gasp and I smirk, knowing my father will take him to task over this later.

I feel something tickling my stomach. Excitement? Nervousness? I've never left Lysan. To be able to see somewhere new beyond the castle grounds and the human villages to the south...

I try to suppress my squeal of delight.

"I will relay this message at once, the king will be most pleased. Thank you, Your Majesties." With another bow he turns to leave the throne room, the great oak doors groaning as they are pulled apart. His black armor clanking with each step, until he pauses just outside the threshold of the door.

"One last thing the king wanted me to impart to all of you." The visitor turns his head; at this distance I can just make out the glow of his red eyes.

"While this night is in the spirit of unity do not mistake us for fools. Anyone found lurking without invitation after the ball finishes will be dealt with by the king personally." A dark chuckle sounds from the stranger's chest.

"Or if you're lucky, one of the beasts that roam Myrkorvin will find you first."

CHAPTER TWO

ELVIE

I CAN COUNT ON ONE HAND the number of times I have been in my father's meeting chambers behind the throne room.

Once, when I was five, I refused to present myself like a lady in front of visiting nobles. My mother had brought me back here to reprimand me. When I was thirteen, Garren and I began to bicker so fiercely at the summer gathering that my father had no choice but to sequester us here until we either came to an understanding or killed each other.

If Garren had had his way it would've been the latter.

It would seem the only time I find myself back here is when I am in trouble. The grim looks my parents and eldest brother are sharing makes this scene feel familiar. I am sat in one of my father's study chairs, bouncing my knee absently. I glance at Briar leaning against the wall, a picture of disinterest.

I feel as though they sense my excitement. How can this not be a marvelous thing? Our two peoples have been separated my entire life. Garren is the only one of us old enough to remember when passage was open between Lysan and Myrkorvin. For that to be the case again…

"I refuse to participate in this," Garren's voice cuts through my thoughts. He levels a golden stare at me. "And you can stop acting like your name day came early. Do you not think people noticed when you perked up at the mention of the ball? How does that make us look to the nobles? That our own princess is intrigued by the prospect of going to those beastly lands. It's abhorrent."

"Oh, now that's a five gold mark word Garren. Abhorrent?" I ques-

7

tion. "And here Madame Oakren said that out of all of us you showed the least passion for language." I rise from the chair, the skirt of my gossamer, gold gown swishing about my ankles, and begin examining the books my father keeps in this study.

My finger coasts over the old leather spines, unsettling the dust accumulated on them. *The History of Lysan: From the Free Magic to King Oxian the First, A Formidable Water: A Comprehensive Guide to Sea Battle, A Perfect Marriage or a Watery Death? Lord Cummings Guide to Selkies…*

My hand finds what I'm looking for and plucks it off the shelf. The leather is soft, the spine folded as though it had been opened and read a hundred times. Judging by my mother's accounts of their courtship, I would not doubt that my father knows this book cover to cover. Walking over to Garren, I slap the book to his chest.

"If being a prince does not work out, brother, I believe you will have quite a career as a poet." He grips my father's copy of *The Lover's Night: A Collection of Love Poems from the Realm,* his fingers turning white. I only smirk as I turn, continuing my glide around the room.

I am restless.

The last time I felt this way was when I took up with the Elves of east meadow and we ran all night through Merrywood forest. Drinking and dancing under the Sun's Moon as it shone full and bright in the sky. Garren had been furious when I was found by the royal guards the next morning. Naked and still high from all the mushrooms we had ingested.

My mother and father had only sent me to my room, where I slept off that evening for half a week.

"This is no laughing matter, and while some weaker-minded males may find your irreverence charming, I find it *abhorrent.*" I smile sweetly at my brother, showing all of my teeth. Garren slams the poetry book on the table and my father cuts him a glare.

"Who is this *king* to make demands of us? We were there during the Orc Wars. This king acts as if we did not also pay a price for those battles."

"King Arkain paid the ultimate price, son. We shall never forget that." My father's voice is calm, sadness tinging some of his words. My mother crosses the room to wrap an arm around his waist. He tucks her head beneath his chin as if the mere closeness of her eradicates all of these thoughts that trouble him.

King Orvian and Queen Mirella of Lysan. The longest ruling monarchs since King Oxian the First. They make a fearsome pair. When I was a child I wished for a love like theirs one day. Not the folklore tales of locked away princesses whose princes saved them from the wicked beasts that lurk in the Merrywood. But of a king who would take one look at me and fall hopelessly in love. Like my father had with my mother.

"We are forbidden from killing, lest we become beasts like them. The king was well aware of that and yet he chose to revoke our people's access to the ancestral lands. This separation has weakened us, Father, you must know what is being said–"

"Enough!" shouts my father. Garren's face goes pale. "What a pack of disgruntled lords think of me is not my concern and it should not be yours either."

"But father—"

"I will hear no more of this. That is not what we are here to discuss." Kissing my mother's head, my father moves to stand next to me. Questions linger in his honeyed eyes as he looks down at me. "Do you wish to attend this ball, my darling?"

I feel myself smiling as Garren rolls his eyes. All good fathers love their daughters the most and mine is no exception. Perhaps it is because I am the youngest. Perhaps it is because he will never have to be strict with me to ensure that I am a good ruler for our people. That he will always just be my father and that's why he treats me this way. Perhaps it is because out of all of us I look the most like my mother but with his rebellious spirit he had to let go of in order to rule.

Whatever it is, there is no denying I am his favorite.

"More than anything."

"Why?" There is no taunt, just curiosity that laces this question.

I take a deep breath. How do I explain myself without sending Garren into a frenzy?

"I'm bored," I hedge. My father raises a golden brow.

"You want to go to Myrkorvin, a land filled with demons and death,

to participate in a night of debauchery and falsehoods because you are...
bored," Garren spits out.

"Why else would someone go to Myrkorvin if not for debauchery? Surely not the stunning views," Briar mumbles, now flipping through the pages of the poetry book Garren discarded.

"I quite like debauchery," I volunteer.

"As do I, but I refrain from saying so in front of Garren as I do not wish to offend the sensibilities of the gentle lady." Briar's head looks up and regards us thoughtfully, mouth twisting into a thoughtful expression. "This poet just rhymed 'look-see' with a female's most intimate parts. Truly, they'll just publish anything these days."

I snort and my father rubs his temples. Though I doubt his headache is solely from the unforgiving metal of his crown. Even in the soft lights of the candles the jewels sparkle like a million stars.

"Very well then, we shall go. As two unmarried and unmated elves you must both participate in the act together. You understand that, don't you? To not do so would be seen as a major slight to the king."

"The act?" Briar puts a hand to his chest, shock widening his eyes. "With my own sister? In this day and age, I thought the elves ended that practice centuries ago."

"The act of The Night of a Hundred Faces, you idiot," Garren snaps. "You do realize you are sending your precious Elveena to the wolves, Father. That if she is chosen by the king or, gods forbid a mate to one of those creatures there is nothing we can do to stop it."

"Elvie won't be anyone's mate and she certainly won't be chosen," my father says.

"Oh, and why is that?"

"Because in all my centuries I have never once heard of a dark and light elf being mates. Light elves mate for companionship, a bond that forms over time together. A way to endure eternity together as your desire for each other grows with each passing year. Dark elves..." My father pauses.

"Dark elves know in an instant. Due to their kind being the result of a light elf taking a life, corrupting themselves by going against our most sacred laws, each generation that was bred loses more and more of themselves to their animalistic side. Dark elves mate for reproductive purposes."

This has turned into a decidedly uncomfortable discussion for all of us.

"A mate to a dark elf is whoever can produce the most powerful offspring. Mating with a light elf would set their children back a generational step. As for being picked as a bride. That, presently, is the least of my concerns about this evening."

"But how can you—"

"So what exactly is The Night of a Hundred Faces? I don't remember reading about it." I cut Garren off before he could speak again.

"They used to be quite common," my mother says. She has been quiet most of this discussion, and I know it is not because she fears speaking her mind in front of my father. No, she has mastered the quiet contemplation and whatever she is not saying now is something that she will impart on us when the time is right.

"When I was a girl my own mother would tell me stories about how Blackfire Castle would host one for its people almost, but as I said before, the tradition ended with the old king. It was thought that he wanted to distance himself from the dark elves being known for the tricks and deceit associated with this act."

"How so?" I ask.

"The act itself is built on deception. From what I can remember of the last one I heard whispers about, it operates much like a masquerade ball. However, when you put on your mask it transforms you completely, magic shuffles you around to disorient you and then you are sent forth. Certain spells and wards are put up to encourage attraction and ensure that your path and your mate's will cross." There is a beat of silence. "With King Arkain using this as a way to find his own chosen bride, the process is the same but at the end of the night the king will bestow his favor to the patron of his choice. Should they accept it then their bargain states they must marry."

"According to their histories, when the first dark elf king was called to select a bride his nobles were killing each other over the prospect of their daughters being selected. Knowing that their kind was fond of tricks, he devised this act to make his decision without any bias and to placate

11

his lords." Nothing says a healthy foundation for a relationship than one built out of deception, right?

"And Arkain's father wanted to get away from all of that. He wanted to stop their people's overreliance on deceit and free magic. For his son to bring this back while also letting us back into Myrkorvin, it is sending a very mixed message."

My mother is right, it does not make a lot of sense. What is his goal with all of this? Surely there is no shortage of dark elf females lining up to be queen. Why bring back this tradition that your own father was so against?

I hear the danger and the warning in my parents' voice and in truth I am a bit wary. The eagerness inside me has not dimmed. While not as fond of tricks, us light elves are cunning. I spoke true to my father. I am bored. Bored of the routine and royal obligations.

One night filled with debauchery sounds like just the thing to lift my spirits.

"It's rumored that the glamor they use makes you the antithesis of what you are. The greater your beauty, the plainer you become." My father's gaze warms my face. "So I fear, my sweet Elvie, that if you manage to keep a low profile, the king's notice will pass right over you."

"What about me?" Briar asks.

"Chin up, Briar. This'll be your chance to see what it's like to be Garren. Maybe it'll help you have some compassion for our brother," I reply primly. Garren rolls his eyes and Briar smirks. My father tries and fails to hide his smile as well. Reaching out a hand he cups my cheek.

"We'll have time to prepare you for this but it's important that you're smart. I know how you like to explore, how trouble always seems to find you, but this isn't going to be like your usual games." He squeezes my face. "They don't play by the same rules."

For the first time since the visitor, came my excitement snuffs out a bit.

"Orvian, she'll be fine." My mother comes up behind me and places a hand on my shoulder. My father nods and takes a step back. They're always like this. Able to convey their thoughts and feelings without uttering a single word. I do not have to turn to know that my mother is responding to the question in my father's eyes. Nodding he turns and sits down at his desk. Opening up a fresh pot of ink and pulling pieces of parchment towards himself, my father begins writing in his elegant script.

"I need to inform the nobles about this development. I have no doubt many of them will be eager to attend."

"And you are going to be late for astronomy lessons. Your tutors keep telling me you're falling asleep in your lessons," my mother's voice grows stern.

"Maybe if Madame Oakren didn't have the disposition of a floundering fish, I wouldn't find myself wishing for a swift death over hearing about the solar system again."

"Regardless, you need to know these things."

"I'm twenty-three, mother, I feel like I am past these lessons. If anything, shouldn't I be learning more about the dark elves? I would hate to offend one without knowing any of their customs." My mother rolls her eyes but my father cuts in.

"She's right. There's lots of things we've never taught them about the dark elves. Never thought they would ever let us pass through the bridge again. They need to be prepared for all of their tricks."

"See?" I can't help but feel a little smug.

"And what, dear husband, is such an important tradition that it should take precedence over your daughter knowing astronomy? Over language and the arts?" My mother places her hands on her hips.

"Here's one that all of you will be wise to remember." My father sets his quill down and levels his gaze at me, the gold burning brighter than before. "No matter what you see. No matter what you hear. Nothing in Myrkorvin is as it appears."

CHAPTER THREE

ARKAIN

IF WYLAN HAD NOT BEEN my parents' advisor I would've killed him by now.

Honestly, I may still kill him if he does not cease his incessant whining. Pacing back and forth in front of my throne, I am amazed that his leather boots have not worn divots into the tile. Back and forth and back and forth he marches. The crimson cloak he wears drapes down his back and drags on the floor.

If I severed his head, his blood would leave a similar trail as it leaked from his neck.

"Once again, my king, I must warn you of what we stand to lose if this ball is to go forward." Wylan turns to me; his crimson eyes are blazing against his gray skin. Scars mar his face, wrinkles show his age. His snow-white hair is long and tangles in the plates of his black armor.

We have not had war since my parents had been slain, yet Wylan still dresses like the alarm could sound at any moment. Not that he would do much more than sit on a hill and wait. He forgets that I was there, fighting beside my father. Willing to die for Myrkorvin like a good prince. A value my father had always instilled in me.

Love is the only thing you should be willing to die for.

My father had died because he loved Myrkorvin enough to charge into battle with too few soldiers. His love for our land had blinded him and made him believe the light elves would be a real asset. When their non-lethal techniques failed, they retreated back into the hills. That love for our land and its people was not enough to save him.

14

Though, I suppose it was my mother's love for him that made her join him in death.

"You have made your displeasure with my choice very clear, Wylan."

I rub my temples to relieve some of the pressure built up there. The black pointed crown I wore had sat atop every dark elf king since the first, passed down from generation to generation. Each one getting further and further away from the light elves we once were descended from.

Our differences rang true on the battlefield. I watched my kind kill, maim, and destroy anything in our path with claws and teeth and vigor. Our latest generation is the most beastly yet. And on the battlefield one can be forgiven if they yield to that side completely for survival.

I myself have been known to do such. "The Beast King," they whisper in the east.

That golden light elf prince had thought so when I watched him flee with the last of our enforcements. Leaving my father to die and for me to turn into something I almost didn't come back from. Now that is something I will never forget.

"Arkain, the light elves have never been permitted to join even when the Night of a Hundred Faces was commonplace. Inviting them to take part now is risky. Not to mention some of the older nobles may see it as a slight to invite our former oppressors to one of our most sacred traditions," Wylan laments.

"The light elves are no longer our oppressors. We have kept them in isolation on their island for centuries, depriving them of The Bridge, and whilst King Orvian is a long-ruling monarch…well even we have heard the whispers of discontent throughout Lysan." I lean back on my throne, the stiffness of the metal pressing against my back. I should have a new one forged, one to better accommodate my size and give me more space, but this had been my father's throne.

"What do I care for King Orvian's popularity? What care should our people have for it?"

"If your report from the east is to be believed and the Orcs are rising again, then we will need them." Standing and stretching the stiffness from my muscles after this morning's rigorous training session, I descend down the dais. Wylan eyes me suspiciously. Every time he has to lift his head to look up into my eyes there is a hint of displeasure. Most likely because he never believed I would grow into a male that would one day intimidate him.

Taking off my crown, I hand it to a servant who rushes to stow it.

"We do not need them. We could easily march over the bridge and have the king and queen beheaded and their children jailed if we wanted to." Wylan places his hands on his hips. "Threatening them with that would be easier than going through all of this nonsense."

"King Orvian is proud and he is established. A man who would rather face death than surrender. Qualities not often found in light elves. A quality he didn't pass to his son it would seem." I sweep my black hair into a knot I wear for training. "We cannot threaten them if we want their help."

"You most of all should know how little help they were in the end."

"But this time they will fight."

Wylan scoffs. "And why is that?"

"Because they'll have something to fight for. Or rather someone."

Turning from Wylan I make my exit from the throne room. These royal tunics are too stiff. Too much embroidery. In situations like these I long for the days of my too-big shirts. Where I had the ability to climb and move unencumbered. Now I feel like every move I make I'm going to rip out of these clothes. They were not meant to contain a warrior's body.

"Someone? Who? Surely not you, Arkain."

I sidestep a few servants passing by. These halls are quiet. Far too quiet. When my parents ruled there was not a day that went by without revelry. Now, I prefer the company of my own thoughts when I am inside. And when they get too overwhelming as they are now, I like the ability to work them off during a training session with new royal guards.

"Not me," I say. Wylan is still in step beside me. "Their princess."

Wylan stops abruptly, almost crashing right into a maid carrying clean dishes.

"Their princess?" He splutters. "What does she have to do with any of this?"

The castle halls are just the same as when I was a boy. Plush red carpets, walls of great black stone. The royal portraits along the wall detail every monarch from the first. Mine will be hung there when I take my queen. As I pass, I notice how much we as a people have changed. From our first dark elf king, Syrin, hair still golden, skin only slightly ashened, and his queen still pure light elf, glowing with that golden light. The last light elf monarch of Myrkorvin.

Until now if my plan goes the way I need it to.

"She, Wylan, is the key piece of this puzzle." Stopping outside my chamber door, I pause and turn to Wylan, his white brows bunched in confusion. "King Orvian would never betroth her to me. But when I select her during the Night of a Hundred Faces, he will have no choice but to part with her. Or deal with the wrath of free magic."

"I still fail to see how this will encourage the light elves to fight. She is a princess. Cattle. Her sole job is to be married off for political gain." Wylan scoffs. "They won't come to our aid if she performs her duty."

My teeth grind together. I grow tired of Wylan's constant questioning. I may not have a mind for politicking like he does, but I do know one thing. How to win a war by any means necessary.

Unfortunately for King Orvian, his beloved daughter has just become that mean.

From all the intel I have received from my spies, Elveena is as beautiful as she is wild. Young. It is…*distasteful* what I am planning to do. The exact sort of thing my father had been trying to steer our kind away from doing. I remember the male he was and I know he would also want me to do whatever I needed to keep our kingdom safe.

And if that means one light elf princess must be tricked into a marriage with me, then so be it. I have withstood worse than a female's displeasure at my actions. If her father found out I was mistreating his kingdom's beloved princess, I'm sure that would spur him and his banner to finally take up arms against us. Not with us.

I may have the soul of a monster but mistreating a female is not something I would ever do. What I planned for her is already bad enough.

And perhaps when the Orcs have been put down once and for all I would consider letting her return home if she wished.

"Cattle? Only a fool would see her as such. Princess Elveena is perhaps the most powerful asset we have for turning the tide with the light elves." We are out of options. Wylan knows this. Opening my chamber door, I hurry inside, stripping out of my tunic and into my training gear. Wylan averts his eyes out of respect or jealousy. I cannot be sure.

The last war decimated our ranks. Our people cannot reproduce fast enough to replenish our stock of soldiers. The ones I am training now have only matured after a century. We do not have that type of time on our side.

If the rumblings of Orc movement from the east are to be believed, then we will need the light elves at our side. The last war stole my family and turned me into a beast. King Orvian will not allow that same fate to befall his daughter. That is why I must marry her. To secure him and his forces.

"I still fail to see how this ruse will gain you more than a young bride. We have not had a light elf queen in almost a millennium. Think of how the people will respond to her."

"They will respond to her better if she is picked during the Night. Seeing it as woven by free magic. No one can argue with its will."

"And you think King Orvian will just let you keep her?"

"He will if he wants to live. A bargain struck in Myrkorvin is a bargain that must be adhered to. And the Night of a Hundred Faces is a bargain weaved between hundreds." Lacing up my boots I stand once more, finding my long sword and strapping it to my hip. "When Elveena is chosen she will have no choice but to submit to our union. And when we call upon the light elves to help us against the Orcs, their *king* will make them. Not out of love for his country but out of love for his daughter, who will be slaughtered should we fall."

"Love is the only thing you should be willing to die for. Applying your father's logic to light elves is risky. They don't love like we do. They don't mate like we do. They're too...*refined*."

Hearing that phrase out of Wylan's mouth sends claws of ice down my spine, but I nod.

"So I get a prudish bride who believes marriages are more akin to eternal friendships. There are worse prices to pay for our people."

"And how will you assure that she is selected? You do understand—"

18

"I grow tired of your questions," I snap. "And of your disrespect. No one questions me. Nor my authority. I keep you because it was what my father willed. It is by my oath to him that you remain here." Wylan's skin lightens a shade as he swallows down his reply.

Brushing past him, I head for the door. The insistent nagging has caused me to be late for the first drills. I need to sweat. I need to hit something and have it hit me back.

"As for the princess," I call back to Wylan who's still standing in my doorway, "she's mine to deal with. Everyone else can keep the fuck away from her."

CHAPTER FOUR

ELVIE

THE CASTLE HAS NOT KNOWN a moment of peace since the messenger left us.

Throughout these past two weeks, the whole kingdom has been buzzing with excitement. Everyone has been permitted to attend, from nobles to servants to humans. From dusk to dawn, Lysan hums with excitement.

Servants whisper to each other in excited voices as they clean. Seamstresses gossip as they sew new dresses for everyone. I've even caught some of the royal guards talking about it, careful to silence all whispering if my brother Garren is to pass by.

After his initial outburst, he has mentioned nothing about the ball. Even though it's the day of, he has been oddly quiet. Perhaps my father's tongue-lashing was enough to stop him for the time being.

I am just as eager as everyone else. I stand on the raised platform inside my chambers as my royal seamstress sews the final touches on my gown . It's pale pink, to bring out the color in my cheeks. Flowing and gossamer, adorned with crystals and jewels and glass butterflies. This is the first ball I have attended since I came of age.

My mother sits in a chair in front of my vanity. She is regal as ever in her long gown that looks like poured gold draped down her body. Her brows are drawn together as she regards me, a million thoughts in her honeyed eyes.

"What do you think?" I ask as my seamstress stows her needle. "And before you say I should've stuck with the royal gold, you know how it makes me look sickly."

My mother huffs a laugh, rising and waving off my handmaids who come to fix my hair.

"I'll do that, you may all go and get ready yourselves. We depart in an hour."

There is a chorus of "thank yous" as each one of them dips into a curtsy before departing. I watch as my mother traces a finger along the curve of the tiara. I never wear them and this one is simple enough. A thin gold wire to encircle my head, adorned with flowers and butterflies made of pearls.

"You look lovely, my dear. Like a true princess." I laugh at that and my mother shakes her head. "It's true. I know how you detest these things. It means a great deal to your father that you agreed, even if you did most of this to annoy your brother."

I smile and mumble, "Not most of it, but that was an added perk." I rub my damp palms on the long skirt of my dress. "Tell me again how this night will go."

My mother sighs and guides me to my vanity table. Sitting down, her long, delicate fingers begin to part and twist my hair. She used to do my hair for me when I was a child. Tonight, it would seem, is special enough to warrant her taking on this task again..

"Like I said before, it has been a long time since the Night of a Hundred Faces was last held. If this new king has stuck with tradition, the act itself is quite straightforward." Picking up a golden pin, she slides it into my hair, holding it back from the side of my face. "Your father and I will present you and Briar as our unmated and unattached tributes to the night. Once you step into the room where it will be held, the free magic will lock you in. It is essentially one big bargain struck between you and the free magic. Only those who are willing to participate will be allowed to. The free magic knows if someone is being forced to participate and the bargain will not work on them. Once the Night of a Hundred Faces commences, you will slip on an enchanted mask that will conceal your true form. The magic will disorient you, and throughout the night you must let it guide you. At the end, if you perform it correctly, you should find your mate or the male you wish to marry and forsake your mating bond in exchange."

While she's been talking, more pins have been secured in my hair. The sections closest to my face have been pulled back, while the long golden length remains curled and flowing down my back. Reaching for the tiara, my mother hums softly.

"I do not know how it will be throughout. Light elves have never participated in this act before and, as you know, the dark elves do not mate like we do. Forsaking a mating bond to them would be abhorrent to their nature."

She's right. In the past two weeks my studies have revolved around the dark elves and Myrkorvin. How their first king spilled blood and corrupted his soul, unlocking a deep well of power that has only seemed to grow stronger with each generation. The corruption spreading and turning their skin dark gray, sharpening their fangs, and growing their once elegant fingers into sharp-tipped claws.

My brother called them beasts and by all accounts he would be right.

Their form should be abhorrent to me. Disgusting. And because of that there must be something wrong with me because I cannot tear my eyes away from their portraits. To wonder what it would be like to lie with one. Something so wild pinning me down and having its way with me.

If my tutors knew the true reason I had taken such an interest in the dark elves they would cease teaching me in a second. If anyone found out how they made me grow damp between my thighs, the nights spent with a hand between my legs as I imagined one of them with me...

He wouldn't be gentle like my previous lovers. He wouldn't touch me with trembling hands or regard me with awe in his eyes. He would use me and own me. There would be no lovemaking, as Lucien insisted we call it.

The dark elf in my fantasy would fuck me. There would be no love found in it.

Perhaps I have been spending a little too much time alone in my room.

"You've gone flush, my sweet, what are you thinking about? If it is about tonight, do not worry. Be smart and be vigilant and this will all be over by sunrise." The golden tiara digs into my scalp. The metal is cold, and looking in the mirror, I almost don't recognize myself. Lysan's one true princess stares back at me.

I need to relax. If we are meant to find dark elves repulsive, then they would surely feel the same about us. It is just the possibility of the unknown that has put me in this state. That has to be it. If my mother knew that it was not nerves over attending this ball that brought color to my cheeks, but rather the wanton thoughts of fucking a dark elf, she would certainly forbid me from going.

As would my father. Garren would drop dead from shame. And if Ryvik thought me a whore before—

Ryvik. A shudder passes through me. He's more monstrous than any dark elf I've studied. Probably more dangerous than them because he disguises it behind a beautiful face. At least what others consider beautiful. Not me though.

Never me.

"Do you ever regret it?" I raise my silver eyes to meet my mother's in the mirror. She still stands at my back, twisting the final strands of my hair around the golden circlet.

Arching a thin brow she asks, "Regret what, my sweet?"

"Forsaking your own mating bond. For dad."

Her hands freeze on my head. We've never discussed this before. Most of our people do not even know that my parents are not mates. That they had both forsaken their bonds in order to be together. I don't know why I'm asking this, tonight of all times, but I want to know.

My mother blinks rapidly and laughs softly, her hands continuing to work my hair.

"I think your father and I were too quick to do so. You know mating bonds between our people are not as quick as those between the dark elves. They can take decades, centuries even, to form."

"So you don't regret it then. Even if there was someone else out there that was supposed to be yours? That your soul was tethered to?"

"All I know is the moment I saw your father, he was what I wanted. For eternity. And if he was not my mate, I would not have another." She finishes my hair and steps back. "Luckily for me he felt the same, if not a bit more...*eager*."

Smiling wistfully, she helps me to my feet. Both of us standing

23

together in front of the long mirror. Mother and daughter. The same face, with the same hair, but with mismatching eyes.

"Who knows, Elvie, now that all of our people are being permitted to participate in the act, maybe you'll find someone you want to introduce to us. So that you can stop sneaking off into town." I snap my head to look at her, my mouth falling open.

Gods damn me, she knows about that?

"Who told you?" If it was Amara the scullery maid who caught me coming back four nights ago with twigs in my hair, I was going to…

"You're not half as clever as you think, my sweet. Besides, I was young once too. I may not have grown up in this palace, but I do understand how stifling it can feel. Especially as you become more curious about *things*." Giving me a knowing look I groan covering my face with my hands.

We are not having this conversation.

I would rather fucking die than have this conversation with her right now.

"No need to get shy on me, Elvie. You're twenty-three years old. A fully matured female. It's natural to have urges you want to—"

"Stop. Please, dear gods, make her stop."

"I'm your mother, Elvie. I just want to make sure you're being safe." My mother gently pulls my hands from my face. She's looking at me expectantly and I know I'm not avoiding this conversation.

"Shouldn't you be mad at me? Disappointed that I didn't stay pure for my wedding night with one of the royal suitors Dad has been lining up for years?"

The quiet stretches between us. If she tells me she is now it'll break my heart. I know some of the courtly ladies whisper about me, it was foolish of me to think she didn't know. Is she ashamed of me and my choices?

Guilt curves my shoulders and I stare down at the marble floor.

A cool hand cups my chin, bringing my eyes back to her warm ones.

"To some males it would matter. But you already knew that."

I give a humorless laugh. "A marriage between me and Ryvik would never have worked for a million reasons. My chastity was the least of them." My mother flicks my nose and chuckles.

"You're right about that. I do not know what your father was think-ing with that." She pauses and I know there is more that she wants to say. She had been silent when the first talks of my betrothal to Ryvik had begun. I remember the stiffness between my parents that I had never seen before. My father's pleading looks in her direction during dinner. My mother's cold stare.

Now it doesn't seem like so much of a coincidence that it was broken off after that initial dinner and my father never raised the subject again.

"So you're not mad at me then?"

My mother smiles and links our arms together as we make our way out of my chambers.

"We live long lives, Elvie. Some spend hundreds of years before they find the one they want to spend the rest of them with. If you are happy and are being safe, then that's all I care about." I roll my eyes and mumble that I'm being very safe.

We pause at the doorway, the hall before us already lined with people in their finery. I can just make out the golden heads of my brothers and father at the far end. Waiting for us to join them so we can begin our journey.

My mother turns to me, cupping my cheek in her hand. Her eyes are open, deep golden pools staring down at me.

"Your father didn't care when it came to me. Who I had been with before…I had doubts that he wouldn't be as understanding. But he didn't care. And I didn't care when it came to him. It was like our lives had begun the moment we locked eyes." She tucks a loose curl behind my pointed ear.

"The right male for you won't care either."

CHAPTER FIVE

ELVIE

THE JOURNEY TO BLACKFIRE CASTLE is a long one.

Gazing out the window of our royal carriage, I watch as the lush greens of our grass give way to rock and sand, the horses of our traveling party lift up their hooves in order to avoid giant rocks that come into our path. The carriage rattles and unease grows in our compartment.

We're getting closer to the bridge.

As the sun dips lower and the oranges and pinks of the sky begin to give way to darkness. The air filtering through the open window turns salty. I lean back from the window and let the ornate curtain, stitched with our royal crest, fall back into place.

Across from me, Garren sits stiff on the bench, his mate Sybil is pressed to his side. Both in our royal colors of golden and red, her light hair twisted at the nape of her neck, showing off its graceful slope. Her golden eyes are wide and taking in everything. They mated after the war so this will be her first time crossing the bridge as well.

If it were anyone else, Garren would chastise them for such open curiosity. Sybil remains the only one that does not ruffle my brother's temperament.

My mother's gown tangles with my own on our side of the bench. Both she and my father made quite a pair as we joined them before our departure. Both regal in their crowns and matching attire. Secret smiles and twinkling eyes.

Now their faces are regal masks hiding secret trepidation.

In fact, the only member of our party who does not seem to be displaying any emotion is Briar. Somehow, even in his stiff finery he manages to look unkempt. Perhaps it is the curl to his blond hair, the hint of mischief dancing in his smile.

"You seem quite relaxed, brother." Garren cuts me a sharp look but I ignore it. Briar's smile turns smug.

"What do I have to be worried about? The king searches for a bride and though I do look dashing in white, something tells me I'm not what he has in mind," he says, cupping a hand under his chin. "I do plan to be a good guest and sample all that Myrkorvin has to offer us tonight. Who knows if we will ever get this chance again."

"What do you mean by 'sample'? Garren says we mustn't consume anything here, for it will be poison." Sybil turns her wide eyes up at Garren, shivering closer to him. I snort softly and Garren glares over the top of Sybil's head.

"It is not poison, my love. But you would do well to avoid it at all cost all the same. Their foul magic corrupts everything," Garren responds, shooting Briar a warning look. "What my brother intends to sample is of a more physical nature."

"A physical nature? What does—"

"Yes, how many are you planning on fucking tonight, Briar? The stable boys are placing bets and I would hate to lose my five gold marks to Skeven again," I say.

A cry of shock goes up between my parents and Garren while Briar doubles over with laughter.

"Enough of this. Elvie, what is the matter—"

"How many did you bet on, dear sister?" Briar asks. "I'll win your coin back."

"Enough. Briar, do not encourage—"

"Well, Skeven said at the last summer party you fucked all of Lord Eldren's daughters by sundown. Fourteen in four hours is quite a feat even for you, so with that in mind, I said you were good for at least twenty-seven—"

"ENOUGH!" My father's command rattles the carriage. His golden skin has turned as red as the rubies on his crown. I have enough self-preservation to look sheepish and Briar is at least smart enough to swallow down his laugh.

"No more talking about bets...or fucking." My fathers glare is hot on my face. "You will behave yourselves tonight. Myrkorvin is dangerous. The dark elves are dangerous. Do not lose sight of this."

"Then why are we even attending?" Garren shoots back. "Why put our people, our family, *my mate*, in unnecessary danger?"

My father opens his mouth but my mother silences him with a hand.

"It is for our people that we do attend. Do not think we are ignorant of the risks. But in the centuries since King Arkain came to power and the Orc Wars have ended, this is the first sign of peace we have been extended by the dark elves." My mother's eyes move around the compartment. Her serious expression has made even Briar pay attention.

"Besides Garren, even you do not know what it was like before the separation. Before we were exiled to our homelands. Our people and the dark elves had an understanding that, as elves, we were all permitted to go to the Kingdom of the Gods. To be able to pray and worship the free magic as is our right." My father sighs, my mother's hand still resting on his arm.

"Being cut off from our ancestral lands is weakening our people. If we ever want to be able to have passage to them again we must first repair our relationship with this new king. If not, I fear what will become of our people—of me—if I cannot lead us back to them."

"What do you mean by that?" Garren asks.

"You must think me a fool if you think I am unaware of what those in the south are plotting." My father gives a humorless chuckle. "An uprising to overthrow King Arkain? To establish the light elf rule in Myrkorvin again? That will not happen in any of our lifetimes."

Garren looks like he has more to say but remains quiet. The creaking of the wheels as we travel more rough terrain is all that fills our cabin.

"So tonight is the first step in unifying our people again? To get back to the way things were before the Orc Wars? Is such a thing even possible?" I ask.

A smile tips my father's mouth.

"That I do not know. What I do know is that there were countless light elf families that lived in Myrkorvin for centuries. Right up until the war, and when the war began those families were ripped apart. Some fled to Lysan, some stayed and helped us in the war effort. I've been thinking for some time that they may be our key to reuniting. To remind him that despite our differences our people used to live and work together. Perhaps King Arkain will be sympathetic towards that and allow free travel again."

"He may be sympathetic if he did not blame us for the death of his own parents," Garren counters. "I saw him that day. His rage at us and at our people. He has not forgotten and he will never forgive."

Based on my studies I find that Garren speaks true. There was so much recorded history of the dark elves that was available before the separation. What happened during the Orc Wars and after that final battle is a bit of a mystery. Some who were there recounted the tale of King Arkain's reign. The arrow that brought down the old king. The queen who had been locked in her own battle letting out a blood-curdling scream before rushing to the dying king's side.

Their love had been recorded in countless tales. Two warriors, mated under a blood moon. Destined to bring Myrkrovin into a new age. Only for the queen to watch the life seep from her beloved mates eyes on that battlefield. The pain of her loss, it was claimed that she died of a broken heart right next to him.

Leaving their son to take up the throne.

More warrior than prince and more beast than elf. Picking up his father's sword he turned into a creature historians were too scared to recount, and made the battlefield run red with orc's blood.

In repayment for our lack of aid, he cursed the light elves from Myrkorvin. Restricting our access to the free magic by way of the Bridge, keeping us to our sunny island. Weakening our people over the centuries.

In all that I had read about him, Arkain was never described as merciful. So why have this party? Unless it was all one elaborate trick, why dangle unity in front of us? What was he planning?

"My hope against all the odds remains the same. That tonight, for whatever reason, King Arkain has entertained the idea of peace between our two peoples." My father clasps my mother's hand and smiles at her warmly. "And this peace will not be kept by a usurper but by a bond no one dares break."

"And what bond is that?" Garren asks.

"The bond of love, of family. Perhaps the king will select a light elf bride, or perhaps he will stay with his own kind. Perhaps he selects no one at all. But his lords will be there. His countrymen. And they will meet someone and fall in love tonight. As is the nature of this evening. Our people, under disguise, will drink and laugh and dance and see that we aren't so different. Just like it was before the war."

I raise an eyebrow but my father goes on.

"The king and his advisors know what is to be gained from this evening. And it goes beyond the simplicity of enacting a royal marriage. It is a test and also an assurance that when the time comes, those who are here tonight will see Myrkorvin as a place filled with beings that are just like us. That will be slaughtered should the Orcs rise again."

"And by that same token, we must use tonight in our favor as well. To secure our people's free passage to the Kingdom of the Gods. To have the free magic strengthen them once more."

Garren opens his mouth again but Sybil places a hand on his arm. The similarity of the gesture my mother is doing with my father now. They stare at each other, communicating in a silent way, and it makes me realize that my mother was right before. She and my father are mates in the same way Garren and Sybil are. There's a familiarity there.

My stomach tightens.

How comforting it must be to belong to someone. Will I ever have that relationship with another? To just look at them and know they belong to me as much as I belong to them?

For as callous and as fickle my brother Garren can be, the only one he is patient with is Sybil. Even now as he looks into her round face, his posture loosens. Leaning down and pressing a soft kiss to her open mouth, it's clear his affections for her is true.

I wrinkle my nose anyways. He's still my asshole brother after all.

"Who knows," Briar says. Obviously the silence has stretched on too long for him. "Perhaps we have the next queen of Myrkorvin in our carriage. Come to unite our people at long last."

My father cuts him a glare and even Garren bristles.

The carriage goes back to being silent and I turn my attention back out the window. Black sky and the whisper of wings from birds overhead are all that I can make out. The lanterns from the side of the carriage cast the night around us in an orange glow.

There is a roaring sound that gets louder with every passing minute. Before I can discern where it's coming from, the carriage jerks to a halt. There is a sharp whistle and then we are in motion again. The roaring is louder now and I realize what it is.

Waves. Crashing against wooden beams.

Rhythmic clacking of the wheels begins as the carriage shakes and moves in sync with it. The bridge. We're really going over the bridge. The horses move with haste as if knowing our welcome here is limited.

The air shifts. Not just from the salt of the ocean but it becomes thicker. Tangier. Metallic. The taste of magic is strong. I feel it hum under my skin.

"I forgot what it felt like, to have free magic," my father says incredulously. I've never felt anything like this before. The power I only scented before I now feel it flowing into my body and dancing at my fingertips.

"How much longer until we are there," I ask.

"Not long enough." Garren has gathered Sybil closer to him even though she seems rapt by what we are seeing outside of the window.

While it feels like an hour has passed, I know it has only been a few minutes when the rattling stops and our carriage is once again on solid ground. My head is fully outside of the window now, the ocean breeze blowing pieces of my hair out of its twist. I cannot seem to take in enough of my surroundings.

Myrkorvin. I am on Myrkorvin soil.

It has the appearance of Lysan but the feeling is different. There is danger here. Even in the darkness of the night, I feel as though I am being watched by a million different eyes. The sensation becomes too much so I fall back inside the cabin, my cheeks cold from the night air. Even Briar has opened his own window and is staring thoughtfully outside.

"Take it in, my children. And remember, this is not Lysan. There are things here that will not hesitate—"

"Your Majesty!" one of our guards calls from the front of the carriage. "We are approaching Blackfire Castle."

Anticipation shortens my breath. A million emotions are rushing through my veins. Myrkorvin. Dark elves. The Night of a Hundred Faces. Things here that will not hesitate…

"Not hesitate to do what, Father?"

The regal mask is back in place. My father is no longer in this carriage but rather King Orvian of Lysan. Queen Mirella is at his side, stoic and strong. The only sign of emotion in him is the softening of his eyes when he regards me.

"Things here will not hesitate to kill you." He turns back to face forward. "The dark elves themselves are at the top of that list. Be vigilant."

Outside the window a war cry goes up. A legion of soldiers in black armor is posted along the road and are the same massive build as the messenger who brought us word of this event. As we roll on I can see it. The inky black tops and bricks are somehow darker than the night sky.

Blackfire Castle.

That feeling of loneliness in my stomach has curdled into trepidation. Our carriage rolls to a stop. The royal procession has also fallen silent. Those in their own carriages are waiting on a cue from us on how to proceed.

The door to our carriage opens. My father exits first, followed by my mother. Then Garren and Sybil. Briar is next and he holds out his hand for me. I hesitate. Isn't this what I wanted? Adventure? To see the unknown? Why are my legs refusing to move?

"Come on, Elvie. The longer you stay in there, the less time I have to bed twenty-seven elves before the sun rises."

I choke on a laugh and place my hand in Briar's. There is a slight tremble and I know it's not my hand that shakes.

I smile at him and whisper, "You know, Skeven said he'd double my bet if half of the elves you fucked were dark elves." Briar laughs and we take our place behind Garren and Sybil as our parents are led into the castle. Soon there is noise from those in our party as they join us in exiting their carriages.

"Well, dear sister, by the time the sun rises I hope to be well and truly satisfied and for you to be ten gold marks richer."

Our father turns to us and we fall silent. A guard dressed in all black with a long cape of crimson approaches from the castle's gate and bows before my father. The wood of the castle door is dark, held together by long rods of black steel. The smell of fire is in the air.

"King Orvian and the Light Elves of Lysan. King Arkain welcomes you to Blackfire Castle and invites you to join in the Night of a Hundred Faces." The guard gestures for us to go through the opening and into the castle.

My father nods and we begin walking, my slippers gliding along the grass. I feel as though I am floating. And for some reason I have this sinking feeling as my feet pass through the archway of the gate that I am never leaving this place again.

CHAPTER SIX
ARKAIN

THE SCENT OF ROASTING MEAT and freshly poured wine is thick in the air.

The halls of Blackfire Castle have not been this loud since the death of my parents. The sounds and smells are almost enough to allow me to feel as though it is years ago. Though the last party I attended I swore would be my last.

Without it, I may never have been strong enough to become who I am.

An old ache forms in my stomach as I look down from my perch along the atrium above the throne room. I'm hidden up here, able to observe what's going on down below. And who is already here.

As a boy I used to hide up here when my parents would invite our lords and ladies to court. When we would have royal visitors that needed entertaining and wanted a taste of our unusual tendencies. I remember how loose my clothes had been on me back then, not like the tight leather that encases me now. So many things have changed since the last ball I attended.

All thanks to her.

Glancing down, I can see the thing that put me on this path. Vysha. Daughter of Lord Vyshen. Her rather callous dismissal of my affections still ring in my ear.

I can hear her cold words of rejection. Her tinkling laughter and the chorus of those around her that joined in to mock what I felt in my heart to be true. Vysha is as beautiful as she is cruel. To have even thought for a moment that she could've been my mate...

34

She looks the same tonight as she did so many centuries ago. Glossy black hair, tight-fitting black gown adorned with hundreds of flaming rubies. They glow with the same fire her eyes do as they scan the ballroom. I guess I am not the only one who changed from that night.

And now I'd rather stick my cock in a razortail's bog than ever make her my queen.

The floorboards to my left squeak. This old atrium has seen better days but it is not a rogue wind causing the disturbance.

"What have I told you about trying to sneak up on me, Aiko?"

Cloaked along the stone wall, a whisper of a laugh tickles my pointed ears.

"If I thought you would actually kill me, Your Grace, you wouldn't even know I was here."

Of that I have no doubt. Aiko is one of the deadliest assassins in Myrkorvin. Perhaps the entire realm if I ever let her out of my employ. Luck had me find her one day in a desolate town on the outskirts of Moonbourne. She had been no more than a halfling babe, I had almost mistaken her for a human.

But no human would have possessed the primal grace to sneak into my saddle bags and rob me of my gold. The town had wanted her killed; apparently I was not her only victim. Whether it was for her status as half dark elf or because she had just robbed their king, I had never seen such fervor for spilling the blood of a child.

So I had given her a choice. I could allow them to carry out her punishment or she could still sneak, steal, and stalk, but this time for me. Aiko has been in my service for the last ten years. And while she has never robbed me again, the gold I keep her flush with for her services guarantee her loyalty and discretion.

"Killing you would put me at quite the disadvantage. Is everything prepared for tonight?"

Aiko pushes off the wall. The glow from the sconces here on the atrium and the moon above give enough light for me to finally get a glimpse of her. The hood of her dark cloak is down, revealing black hair the color of ink pulled back from an angular face. The only indication that she has any dark elf lineage is in the slight pointing of her ears.

One of her parents must have hailed from the eastern lands beyond the Brokenbone Mountains. The even gold hue to her skin glows underneath the pale moon. Her dark eyes assess me, missing nothing.

"Everything is prepared. The guards have been made aware of the plans. They have been briefed on what to expect as far as this whole *ball* goes."

I chuckle at that.

"And why are you not dressed for the ball, Aiko? My direct order for you was to keep an eye on our friends from the south."

"Do not insult me, my lord. I do not need a mask to conceal me; if I do not wish to be seen, then I shall not be seen. As far as our friends from the south." She looks down from the railing to the party guests trickling in. "The King and Queen of Lysan as well as their three children have arrived for the party."

I grip the banister, the old wood creaking under my fingers. Tonight is a means to an end, nothing more. These wounds I have spent centuries trying to heal, yet at the mere mention of the King and Queen, it is like I am back on that battlefield. Swords clanging, my mother's wailing, my father's blood soaking through my armor…

A golden knight perched atop a white stallion, only to turn and flee.

Aiko slides closer to me, raising a brow at my sudden change in demeanor.

"At the risk of inciting more of this sudden wrath that will surely lead to the defacing of our historic atrium, I should caution you to not look down at the guests who are entering in…three…two…*one*."

I cannot help myself and I glance at the palace room before me. The light elves have arrived. Flowing golden gowns, silver hair, skin as pale as the moon above. They fan out within the room, eagerness and morbid curiosity written on their faces. Golden eyes are wide as they take in the castle. As they feel what it is like to live with the free magic once again.

And then there he is. The Cowardly Golden Knight.

The banister I'm gripping snaps in half, splinters cut into my palms, the metallic scent of my blood perfumes the air. A few elves below snap their heads up but we are concealed up here. Aiko lets out a soft curse and slinks back into the shadows.

The King and Queen continue their descent. Floating with that practiced grace of light elves. The coward, Garren, follows closely behind them. A pretty prince. A mirror of his parents in front of him with an elegant light elf draped in matching gold clinging to his arm. The closeness, the way he curls her closer to his side, the way his eyes travel about the room assessing everything for any threat that it could pose to her.

It seems while I inherited a kingdom and an empty castle, Garren has found himself a mate.

My teeth grind and I'm about to call off this whole thing and leap down below. To use my hands and snap the prince's neck. To let his mate wail over his corpse as my mother did to my father's. To enact revenge on the light elves like I have dreamt about each night.

I can feel myself doing it, my muscles tensing, coiling, ready to launch me into action.

Before I can move, though, something stops me. No not something, *someone*.

The most beautiful creature I have ever seen. With dread curdling my stomach, I know she can only be one person. She looks just like her mother who has just passed, though her face has a delicate softness. There is a curiosity that lights up her silver eyes. They are not the cold amber typical of Lysan's royal family.

Draped in her gossamer dress, a sparkling tiara tucked into the flowing locks of her white hair, Princess Elveena, has rendered me immobile. I am powerless to do anything but watch her as she follows behind her brother. Those eyes taking in the sights of my palace.

I find myself wanting to know what she thinks of it and cursing myself that I have let some of it fall into disrepair. She does not seem frightened. And as I remember what my plan is for tonight I think this is at least some small miracle.

Being so rapt by her, I barely notice the male she's walking arm in arm with. The anger that she had first quelled after I saw Garren was now back in full force. Who is he? Why is he touching her? Is she *mated*?

That thought has me almost jumping off the banister again. Until I get a glimpse of the male in question. And the family resemblance is quite clear. That allows my blood to cool again.

What is happening to me? What has caused me to act like this?

Perhaps I am more animal than I had thought. These years in solitude doing little more than training for the next war have perhaps robbed me of the last traces of my civility.

The beast inside of me becomes even more apparent as Princess Elveena continues to walk throughout the room, the black mask needed for tonight's affairs dangling from her slender fingers. Her gown hugs her slight curves so perfectly, the material so thin that I can just barely make out the curves of her breast. As she passes under the atrium and continues forward, the sheets of the gown part just slightly, revealing the smooth, pale expanse of her thigh.

The blood that was roaring in my head a moment ago has now traveled south. I cannot remember the last time my cock has been this hard for anyone. Even after a battle, when bloodlust was high, it was never like this. It never transformed me into a beast wearing an elf's skin.

But that is what she has done to me. Wishing only to know if the soft pink of her lips matches the delicate nipples she is hiding beneath her gown. If her thighs will feel as soft as they look when I am nestled between them.

Guilt sours those thoughts.

She is a light elf after all. A royal. A princess. Who has been taught, I am sure, to view my kind as lesser, as monsters. She will scream at the sight of me, not welcome me into her bed with a serene smile. Especially with what's to come tonight.

Of all the things I will have to do to Princess Elveena, forcing myself on her will not be one of them. The thought of her in any sort of distress does something funny to my stomach. Something I will not be examining any closer.

I cannot let whatever this is distract me. The plan tonight must go off without a hitch, lest my realm be doomed to fall.

Pushing away from the banister, I make my way down the stone steps. Before the night is over I will be much closer to Elveena and I cannot let whatever feelings those were rule me. I have to be smart, I cannot fight my way out of this one.

"Everything is in order with the masks?"

Silently, Aiko has fallen in step behind me on the stone stairs. The leather of my boots echoes off the wall while Aiko's breathing is the only sound to know she is with me.

"They are just as you instructed. Tricks and all. They'll be starting soon, so here." Aiko goes to hand me one of the black masks the guests will be wearing to take part in the Night of a Hundred Faces, but I wave her off.

"I won't be needing that," I say, cracking my neck and holding back the unease coursing down my spine. It's only for a little bit, I remind myself. A temporary discomfort, nothing more. Exiting the stairwell, I pause. Aiko hangs back in the shadows and I grin. Though her face is hidden, I sense she is rolling her eyes at my attempt of bravado.

"For what I have planned tonight, I'm going to use something a bit stronger than a cursed mask."

CHAPTER SEVEN

ELVIE

BLACKFIRE CASTLE IS JUST AS ominous as the forest that surrounds it.

As soon as my feet crossed over the threshold into the great hall, I could feel the change. Not only in the air around me, but within myself as well. The other highborn elves linger close to me and my parents. Still too afraid to venture too far out from the pack.

But I know they feel it too.

I am weighed down by the strength of the magic in the air. Its metallic scent assaulting all of my senses. My body feels like I have just drunk a barrel full of our sweetest wine. This power is intoxicating and all-consuming.

In Lysan, I am no more powerful than a typical elf. My father wields a great deal but the separation from the free magic after all of these years has weakened him. Now as I look towards him, it is as if he has doubled in size.

The warmth of his magic is radiating off him like warm rays of sun. His silver hair glowing with power. His eyes are glowing as if he has been lit from within. My father was never a slight man, but standing next to my mother, is it just my imagination or is his chest more robust? Has my mother's head always just barely grazed the underside of his chin?

Even Garren and Briar seem to be glowing and strengthening before my very eyes. Glancing down at my hands, I have to assume I am as well, my pale skin is a stark contrast to the ominous black mask dangling from my fingers.

Procuring this was most awkward. The servant who handed me this mask had the strangest look on her face that I still cannot place. I shake myself out of those thoughts and keep in step with Garren at my side.

His eyes scan the room, taking in the figures around us. So much gray skin and red eyes. Even after weeks of studying them, nothing could have prepared me for the sight of them in front of me. It is hard to tell that we were once the same kind. If their outward appearance did not highlight the difference, there is an animalistic aura that surrounds them.

Countless pairs of red eyes appraise us from behind gold-encrusted wine goblets. Elongated fangs glinting in ferocious smiles as we pass them and reach the center of the throne room. I am shocked by my lack of fear. It is obvious to me that we have built the dark elves into these creatures of the night they clearly are not.

Different does not always equate to beastly. Perhaps, though, I am the only one who thinks this way, as I watch one of Lord Sunwyne's daughters nearly faint as she brushes against a dark elf guard.

We cannot all be critical thinkers.

"So," Briar whispers next to me, "twenty-seven? And if over half are dark elves, is Skeven really going to double your bet?"

A laugh leaves my lips. "Is that doubt I hear? Are you worried your usual charms won't appeal to them?"

"Dear sister, how you wound me with your lack of confidence. Believe me, if King Arkain were a queen I would've had our two countries reunited after one pleasure-filled night. No female—human, elf, or otherwise—can resist me when I make my affections known." His smile at me is all teeth, glinting in the candlelight from the sconces along the wall.

"And so humble too, brother. You truly are a gift to females throughout our realm."

"That's what they tell me when my head's between their—"

"Be quiet, you two!" Garren's blond head whips around, shooting dangers from his eyes at us. Briar tries to smooth his laughter with a hand but it is to no avail. We've stopped moving now. We are lined up facing a dais and an ominous black throne looms in the center of it. It seems to be constructed from the same black stone that the castle is made from.

Looking around, both light elves and dark elves regard each other warily. It has been an age since our two people were in the same room. There is an unease that permeates the room. Maybe it is the guards armed to the teeth that stand at each exit. Once we have all filtered inside, the great oak doors slam shut with finality.

But not before a figure sneaks in.

Moving silently on the polished stone floor, I can just make out the figure of a young male. Perhaps no taller than me, slight with glowing red eyes that are too big for his face. His clothes are nice but far too big for his skinny frame. Black hair falls down his neck and slightly over his face. He looks too out of place compared to everyone in their finery.

Yet no one besides me seems to notice his arrival.

I turn my head to ask Briar if he sees the youngling only to be greeted by open air. I narrow my eyes and see Briar chatting to one of Lord Alderred's daughters. He looks over at me over her dark hair and winks and I simply shake my head.

Looking back, I have lost sight of the figure.

In fact, it seems I have lost sight of everyone I came with. My mother and father are no longer beside me and neither are Garren and Sybil. The smell of magic has begun to intensify, my head is feeling light whilst my body feels too heavy to move.

Instead of going in search of my parents, my feet feel glued to the tile beneath me. The candles along the wall flame brighter. The sound of heavy boots pounding the ground intensifies until the door next to the dais is thrown open. A line of imposing dark figures enter the room and line up in front dais. Each one is completely obscured by their own dark cloaks except for one.

A white-haired dark elf takes his position at the front. He is older, lines of age are deep along his eyes and forehead. A prominent scar runs along the side of his face. His black armor is adorned with gold markings indicating his rank is of importance. His red cape is held at his shoulders and detailed with matching golden thread.

This must be Wylan, Advisor to the King, if my memory serves from my lessons.

"Good evening, dark and light elves alike," His deep voice booms across the hall. All chattering has stopped as red and gold and silver eyes turn towards him on the stage. "It is the pleasure of King Arkain, Ruler of Myrkorvin and the Dark Elves, to welcome you to Blackfire Castle as we come to celebrate and participate in our longstanding tradition of the Night of a Hundred Faces. May the First Gods smile on us tonight and bless the unions that will be forged this evening."

A pair of dark elves in front of me whisper to each other. Their dark gowns match the inky color of their hair. I crane my neck forward to try and hear them better.

"Which one do you think is the king?" the one on the left whispers.

"Second from last, I saw him perform at the tournament last summer and I'd recognize his build anywhere."

I drag my eyes back to the stage. How they can even discern these figures apart, I have no idea. If I get selected by a dark elf tonight then perhaps it is a good idea to learn how to tell them apart.

That idea rocks me. I am not staying here. When the night is over I shall return back home. So why does that thought sadden me?

"The rules of the Night are simple," Wylan continues. "If you are selected by our king, he will bestow his favor on you. At that point you will have to state that you wish to stay. A bride achieved during the Night cannot be someone who is forced. This night is a bargain that both parties must agree to. Is that understood?"

There is a chorus of agreements and Wylan continues his speech.

"For the rest of you, this Night is not simply for King Arkain to find a bride. But rather a chance for our people to reacquaint themselves with each other. Our sisters, while you may hope to end this evening a queen, you may end it with a new friendship, lover, or for a lucky few of you, perhaps even your mate is in this room. May the free magic guide you to them."

Wylan nods and the figures on the stage bring forth their hands that were clasped behind their backs. Identical black masks are in their hands that match the ones in ours. Slipping them onto their faces there is a sudden burst of white light. A few in the crowd gasp as we watch it occur.

Towering figures are transformed. Still elves but no longer dark elves. The one on the end that was the largest of the bunch has been turned into a lean figure a good foot shorter than himself. With brown skin that glows under the candlelight and a close cut beard of dark coiled hair. The rest of his dark hair is braided back from his face, revealing a strong jaw and amber eyes.

The rest follow this transformation in turn.

"These masks will change your appearance to those around you. When I give the signal, please put on your mask and let the free magic guide you. Once the dawn begins to rise, everyone will return to this throne room. Once we are all back inside you will be permitted to remove your masks. Should the king have selected a bride, she will remain here from this night forward."

Sweat slides down my spine. I know my father said the chances of me being selected were slim. Just keep to myself and all will be well. Besides, I'd much rather explore than mingle. A chance to move freely without the watchful eyes of royal tutors or my brother sounds like something I have been longing for. The chance to explore this place to its fullest before I'm sent back to live in Lysan for the rest of eternity.

"The castle will be open to all of you. But be cautious of exploring. The King guarantees your safety within these walls, but should you leave them"—Wylan pauses—"the monsters who call the surrounding woods home are nothing short of nightmares. Now please, put on your masks and let the night commence."

I hesitate and stare down at the black mask. There is no turning back once I slip this on. Without giving myself a chance to reconsider, I push the mask over my nose and I am plunged into darkness just as a cry goes up.

The metal smell burns my nose and coats my teeth. I grind my teeth against the feeling of magic ripping against my skin. The discomfort is brief before my vision returns. I am outside the throne room. I look down and my pink gown is replaced by one of a drab brown.

Patting along my sides and breasts, I definitely feel different. Fuller of chest and rounder of hips. I glance around me and see that I am alone in the hallway. Interesting. Following the sound of voices, I make my way along the corridor.

Royal portraits hang along the wall. Centuries of dark elf kings and queens stare down at me until I find what I need. A mirror framed in silver. The sight before me steals my breath. I feel the same, if only a little lightheaded from all the magic.

But staring back at me is a stranger. One with shoulder-length brown hair and brown eyes. A smattering of freckles cover my nose and chin. The slight point to my ears is the only indication I am not completely human.

There is laughter behind me as a group of other female elves pass. I open my mouth to speak to them but they ignore me. Completely. As if I am no more than a fixture on this wall. No pausing, no curtsying. A laugh escapes me.

Finally, I am invisible.

I am not Princess Elveena of Lysan. I am an ordinary elf. Another giggle threatens to burst out of me when I notice something down the hall. A door is slightly ajar and I can see the hints of pale moonlight. I cannot be chosen by the king if I avoid the party altogether. My thread-bare slippers snag on the red carpet as I make my way to it.

I pass by a few more elves locked in conversation. There is already a pair of dark-haired elves kissing behind one of the columns. Lips on throats and hands wandering down the front of trousers. None of them notice me as I pass and I keep going until I reach the door.

The ornate Myrkorvin sigil is carved into the dark wood. With a sigh, I push open the door and am greeted by cool night air. The moon above is silver and surrounded by a bouquet of stars. Making my way down the stone steps, I giggle and spin, my brown gown dragging behind me as the hem is soaked through by the dew on the grass.

Wind threads through my dark hair and though I am not myself, I have never felt more like myself in my whole life. Invisible. Ordinary. A chance to be free. To just be. I keep spinning in the grass until I am dizzy and collapse to the ground with a smile. The stars above shine on my face as I take deep breaths. The floral scent of night blooming flowers tickles my nose.

Alone. Free and alone at last. What am I going to do first—

A twig snaps next to me and I shoot up into a sitting position. The slight figure from earlier stands in front of me with hands on his hips.

I raise an eyebrow at him as he continues to look down at me before opening his mouth.

"You really shouldn't be out."

CHAPTER EIGHT

ELVIE

"DID YOU HEAR ME?" THE young dark elf asks again. "You aren't supposed to be out here."

"You're out here," I counter, rising to my feet and brushing the grass from my hands. In my new body I am just slightly shorter than him. But still tall enough to look at him in those ruby red eyes. He did not use a mask to camouflage himself so he must not be participating in the Night.

"The rules don't apply to me," he says, crossing his arms. "Besides, you'll miss out on all the mingling if you stay lying on the ground like this. That's what this ridiculous night is about after all, isn't it?" He raises two dark eyebrows at me, daring him to challenge him on this.

How interesting.

"What do you care if I miss my chance? Besides, I'm sure your mother is looking for you." I make no move to return inside. I start down the stone path that leads towards a dark garden. The night is so calm and Wylan only warned about going into the forest

My evening friend bristles and narrows his eyes at me.

"Believe me, elf, I am much older than I look. I am probably a lot older than even you." I huff at that and continue my walk.

"I am not much in the mood for mindless mingling. So you have two choices: to leave me on my evening stroll or to engage me in more interesting conversation."

He hesitates for a moment and something passes over his features. Seeming to realize I've asked him a question, he falls in step beside me.

"If you have no interest in fraternizing then why did you participate

46

the Night of a Hundred Faces?"

I hesitate, almost saying that it was my royal duty to attend. But in this body I can be anyone. My troubles as Princess Elveena do not trouble the vessel I currently inhabit.

"My father made me." It's not a total lie.

We continue down the stone path to the garden. An archway made of gray stones is up ahead. It is coated in wisteria that is growing up its sides like veins. Even at this distance from the entrance, I can already smell the fresh blossoms that are housed there. What type of plants grow in Myrkorvin? Surely some wild and unpredictable things.

My companion has grown silent next to me. That simply will not do. If I am to travel in silence then I will travel alone.

"I saw you before Wylan began his speech. Sneaking into the throne room like an assassin." I cut him a glance and he raises a dark brow at me. "Why did you not put on a mask if you are as old as you claim?"

He laughs but it holds no humor.

"I think my natural face would be enough to dissuade my fated mate should she be lurking here tonight."

That draws me up short and I stop under the garden arches and turn to face him. Noticing my expression, he stops next to me.

"Do not speak about yourself that way." There is a sadness to my companion. One I should have noted earlier. His shoulders curve inward, as if he is trying to shrink his already slim form. What has caused him to believe this about himself? Sure he is young and frail, but there is a gentleness to his face. It strikes me as odd that my kind regards his as beasts, when he is no more than a skittish cub. In truth his face is quite appealing and whoever has caused him to feel otherwise about it should be disgusted with themselves.

"You are quite handsome, my nameless companion."

He gives me an incredulous look as we pass into the garden.

"Besides, who else would show me night blooming blossoms? Albeit unknowingly. And you have intrigued me, which makes you more interesting than half the people I've ever met."

I leave him standing there with raised eyebrows, the night wind blowing his tunic softly.

47

The garden is magnificent. As light elves, our magic is used for protection and healing. My specialty is with plants. The sheer number of plants here that I've only read about makes me gasp in awe. The *night-blooming lotus* of the eastern plains with its purple petals and white centers. The *darksky rose* that comes from the base of the Brokenbone Mountains with its magenta petals.

I could spend hours here. It would take me that long just to see all of the wonders this garden holds.

I stroke the black petal of a *deadman's rose* and watch it curve around my finger. My power tingles and with some concentration I will it into the plant. Watching as it shivers and shimmers until its petals become engorged and double.

My companion has come up behind me and regards me and the *deadman's rose* with raised brows.

"How did you do that?"

"It's my power. Healing, but mainly with plants. I can feel their energy and they can feel mine. What about your magic?"

"Nothing like that, I assure you." I turn away from the plant and he follows me deeper into the garden. "Why don't you want to go back to the party and be with the others again?"

"In truth, my mysterious friend, royal functions bore me."

We walk deeper into the garden. A stream is there, slow-moving water that is as dark as the night sky above.

"What about you and royal functions? Or is this your first one?"

He looks down at the stream and tucks his hands into his pockets.

"Unfortunately, this is not my first one. They're always just like this though."

"Dreadfully dull? Have you ever met the king?"

"King Arkain?"

"Yes," I say. "I hear he is quite the formidable figure. I should like to see him at least, but the incessant chatter of a royal party holds very little appeal to me."

"The king is very private. Many in Myrkorvin were shocked that he ordered this."

TAKEN BY THE DARK ELF KING

"Do you think he'll pick a bride?"

My companion regards me closely as if deep in thought. Something lights in his ruby eyes.

"Perhaps, if the Night goes according to plan," he answers

"If the free magic deems it, you mean?"

"Something like that." He looks over his shoulder and sighs. "I want to show you something."

"Oh?"

"Since we're already breaking the rules by being in here, you can't leave without seeing the best part." His slender hand wraps around my upper arm as he leads me deeper into the garden. I do not fear my companion. There is an honest quality about him that has made me lower my guard. I have to admit his hand on my arm is a pleasant feeling. His touch is gentle but firm as he guides me down the rows of flowers and hedges.

My slippers snag on the roots below but my companion stops me after a few minutes. We've entered a secluded clearing near the back of the garden. It is no wonder this place is so far removed from the others. In the middle sits the most marvelous willow I have ever seen. Ancient roots have grown all through the grass. Branches covered in glowing petals drape down.

A *dawn's willow*. My breath is stolen as I take in its imposing form. They were supposed to be extinct yet here one sits. Proud and basking in the moonlight overhead.

"My mother used to bring me here when I was younger." I turn to face my companion. "This was her favorite part, and with the way your face lit up at the *deadman's rose* I knew you would like this too."

I am at a loss for words.

"This is…wonderful. Thank you—" I stop myself and cover my mouth. "Oh gods, I do not even know your name."

My companion chuckles as we walk closer to the willow. The glowing branches cast his gray skin in a lovely hue. Monstrous? No. He is just like me. Two beings appreciating the natural wonders the gods gave us.

"You can call me Ari."

"Ari," I smile as I test the name on my tongue. "Call me El."

He smiles, blunt fangs glinting. Looking into his eyes I feel hypno-

49

tized by them. By the kindness he has shown me by sharing this part of himself with me.

We stay beside the willow. Ari picks some of the wildflowers at its base while I stroke a finger up and down the hanging branches. I can hear the willow singing to me with every pass. Obviously the king or the royal gardener has been neglecting her. If I were to stay here I would not make the same mistakes.

Staying here. There's that thought again.

That perhaps it wouldn't be so bad to remain. To be chosen and live out my days here in this garden, tending to the plants that are clearly in need of a kind hand. And if the dark elves are more like Ari than the monsters we have been told, Myrkorvin wouldn't be so bad then.

I stop my touching and look at my companion. The gentleness I saw in him earlier has only solidified as I see him with the flowers in his hands. That gentleness causes my stomach to feel funny. I was not lying before, he is quite handsome. Even more so now after showing me the willow.

His head snaps up and he looks back towards the castle.

It is then that I hear it. Music carried on the wind. It is faint but I can just make out the notes of a slow dance. Ari turns back to collecting his flowers but not before I see it. The look on his face. Loneliness. And longing. That is what has me moving towards him.

Ari is the only being I have come into contact with tonight that is not hiding behind a mask. That even with his self-doubts he would rather be his true self than hide behind an enchanted mask. That warms my heart towards him even more.

"Have you ever danced at a ball, Ari?" I ask.

His dark head snaps towards me, a few flowers dropping from his hands.

"No, I tried once but…" He pauses. "Let's just say it didn't go as smoothly as one may have hoped."

"But you know how to dance?" I ask. He nods his head and the skin on his cheeks darkens slightly. He is blushing. How adorable.

I hold out my hand and he looks at it like it's a snake ready to strike. Without giving him a chance to back away, I snatch his hand and pull him close to me. His body is pressed close to mine and the last flowers in his hands float to the ground.

"Then you'll have no problem leading me in this dance then?"

"Are you sure?"

"Yes, think of it as my way of saying thank you for showing me the willow."

He nods, and as if reluctantly, his hand comes up to rest on my waist. His fingers curve slightly and my heart beats faster. He grips my hand tighter and then we are moving. Even with the clear uncertainty on his face, his steps are precise as he guides me through the dance. We twist and spin in time with the faint music from the castle.

My skirt catches on the grass which is surely leaving behind stains. His hand grips my waist tighter and our bodies fit closer together. Looking up into his eyes they have lost that guarded quality. Rubies shine down on me and I smile at him in return.

We dance around the willow, being carried on an invisible wind. As the song comes to an end, so do we, laughing and breathing heavily at the base of the magnificent tree once more.

"That was—" I begin.

"Amazing," Ari cuts me off. His chest moves up and down with his deep breathing. "Thank you for that. Truly."

I smile at that and wink.

"Don't mention it." I pause. "But we aren't done yet."

His brow furrows. "What do you mean?"

"This was just a test to make sure you knew how to dance properly at a royal ball." I laugh. The sky above is turning pink. How long have Ari and I been out here? "You still need to actually dance at the ball."

His features are skewed up in confusion and then it dawns on him.

"Oh, no. You can't be serious," he says.

"I'm afraid I am. Deadly serious." Snatching his hand back, I drag him away from the glowing of the willow and towards the roar of the castle.

CHAPTER NINE

ELVIE

EVERYONE IS STARING AT ARI and me when we enter.

I would like to think it's because he is not concealed by glamour like the rest of us, but in my heart I know it is because of the pair we make. I pay them no mind but Ari hesitates. I tug him after me with my head held high. These elves are no better than him or me.

The music is louder now that we are back in the throne room. The men who were up on the dais earlier in the night are being engaged by ten to twelve elves each. I hope one of them is the king. That way my evening spent away from the party was not for nothing.

And it was special thanks to Ari.

We cut through the crowd towards the dance floor and Ari tugs on my hand.

"How can you stand it?" he whispers.

"Stand what?"

"All of the staring?"

I glance back at the crowd and they are still looking at us. I do my best to glare and pull Ari closer to me. Who are they to judge? They think they are so powerful with their true forms hidden. It is ridiculous.

"These beings here are no better than you or I. They would do well to remember that. Believe me Ari," I say as we cross onto the dance floor. "You have something they could never have."

"What's that?" He asks, his skin turning a sickly pale gray.

"Kindness. None of them would've shown me the willow." I look around the room. "And honestly, you're braver than them by staying true to yourself. You should be proud, not cower under their stares."

"And you are not embarrassed to be seen with me?"

"Embarrassed?" My tone is incredulous. "Ari, I am proud to be with you. We are at the very least friends now. Wouldn't you agree?"

He's quiet for a moment then nods. "Yes, friends."

"And as my friend, allow me to impart some wisdom on you that I have learned over the years. If they don't like you, fuck them. If they do like you then *fuck* them too." Ari's scarlet eyes go as big as saucers at my coarse language. I smirk and take his hand and guide it to my waist. "Now, my newfound friend, let us dance and forget about all of them."

Before Ari can say anything else I pull us onto the floor and we are swept up into the music. The polished tiles squeak under our feet as we turn through each song. I spin, Ari spins with me. I twirl, Ari catches me. Around and around we go through each dance.

I am sweaty. Soaking through my threadbare gown, my dark hair sticking to my face but I do not stop. Those around us keep in time with the music. The elves once staring have returned to their conversations. The band keeps up. Playing song after song after song, Ari and I dance through each of them.

The free magic, Myrkorvin, or maybe just Ari himself makes me feel light. Like I am drunk on berrywine and my feet move without my urging. The fast-paced dances keep us going. Around and around we go, never slowing and certainly never stopping.

I do not know how many songs we have danced to until a slow one comes on. Ari and I come together to catch our breath. We haven't stopped dancing, like the two of us are unable to. There is something pulling me towards Ari and that's what keeps me wanting to dance with him. To not stop dancing even as my feet beg for relief.

"Aren't you tired?" Ari asks me as we dance slowly together.

"Exhausted, but why does that mean we should stop?"

He laughs at that and the sound warms my heart.

"I've never met anyone like you El," He says.

"I should certainly hope not."

Slowing down but still swaying with the music, he takes his hand from my waist and digs in his pocket, producing one of the wild flowers from the base of the willow. It's a beautiful pale pink that almost matches the gown I was originally wearing.

"May I?" he asks and I nod. He tucks it gently behind my ear and I swear I can feel his finger lightly caress the shell of my ear. I smile at him and feel my face heat before pushing up on my toes to kiss him softly on the cheek. I watch as his face darkens; it's only fair that he's blushing too.

We continue to sway softly as the final cords are struck and the hall is plunged into silence. Ari opens his mouth as if to say something but is cut off by the thundering of wooden doors opening.

The white-haired dark elf is back. Wylan, flanked by a legion of royal guards. A few gasps go up and I find myself reeling. This night has flown by for it to be at an end. I look to Ari, whose eyes bore into me as if...pleading?

This is it for us, isn't it? The thought sours my stomach. If only we had had more time. He's the most interesting creature I have met in awhile. But soon I will be unmasked and forced back across the bridge to live as a protected princess.

And what is to become of Ari? I reach out and squeeze his hand.

"I wish we had more time," I say, hurriedly.

His lips tip at that. "You'd want to stay in Myrkorvin for me?"

The hall has grown so quiet you could hear a pin drop. Wylan has assumed his position at the front of the dais, long red cape flowing behind him. I squeeze Ari's hand again and nod, my heart thundering in my chest.

I would stay here for a chance to know Ari. For a chance to break with my routine. At only twenty-three, how can I already be bored of a life I am supposed to endure for eternity?

"I know there are more places you could show me. I wish I could stay here and see them all." With one final squeeze, I drop his hand and turn to face the stage.

All the elves around me have turned too. A few of them are paired off. I wonder how my brother fared this evening after being robbed of his good looks. If he kept good on his boasts I'll at least have some gold marks waiting for me back at home.

Idly, I think about the king. If he found someone during this night or was this risk to his kingdom's security for nothing? Perhaps my father is right, that this was merely for show. In hopes that enough of our kind would see that Myrkorvin and the dark elves that inhabit it are just like us. That if anything, this has pushed us towards being closer once again.

Without having the free magic so abundant, it will be hard going back and seeing what little my powers can do.

"Thank you all for participating in the Night of a Hundred Faces. In a few moments I will ask that you remove your masks. Some of you may be shocked to find out who you spent the evening with." I glance next to me and see Ari and smile. For some reason he doesn't return it, just keeps looking straight ahead. I chalk it up to just being nervous and return my attention back up front.

"King Arkain hopes that this evening will go a long way in showing both our kinds that there is still some commonality between us. That if we can dance and laugh together, that our relationship can be restored." Wylan looks over the crowd one final time, eyes catching on something but he quickly disregards it. "You may now remove your masks."

With a deep breath I reach up and feel the invisible lip of the mask. It takes some force but I pry it off and watch as it clatters to the ground. I am back at my true height. I can feel my long hair tickling down my back. My gossamer gown flowing down my legs once more.

There are light elves and dark elves around me. A few look stunned to see who they were just linked in arms with. The pair of elves I saw kissing along the columns are two light elves from one of our southern territories. They smile at each other and kiss.

How sweet.

I raise my arms above my head, stretching with a yawn as all the dancing catches up with me. One final metallic smell hits my nose and that's when it happens. A female dark elf turns towards me with a look of shock as she gasps and points.

My time at being invisible was short-lived. Truth be told I've never experienced that sort of reaction before, even when I first walked in with my family in the whole royal procession. She's not the only one to act this way. The whole of the hall turns and gasps at me. Even light elves, which I find very odd.

Surely they are used to seeing me.

Until I realize it is not me they're gasping at but the figure behind me. Ari. What about him has elicited such a response? There is an anger building in me. I know light elves can be cruel when it comes to outward appearance, but Ari is my friend and to have him be greeted with this abject horror…

But it isn't horror on their faces. Nor is it disgust. It is surprise? As if they cannot believe what they are seeing. Everyone in the hall has turned, even Wylan on the dais has narrowed his eyes to Ari who is behind me.

Slowly I turn myself, hoping that when Ari realizes who I am he will still wish to be friends. That Elvie the princess is just as wanting of his friendship as El the common elf.

"Ari, why is everyone staring at us…" I begin before trailing off.

Ari is no longer behind me. No trace that he ever was there but the flower I can still feel tucked behind my ear.

Where my friend stood before now houses a hulking figure. He is massive. Easily a foot and a half taller than me. His black leather armor is stretched tight over rippling muscles and wide shoulders. The adornments on his breastplate double Wylan's and his red cape is twice as long, spilling out behind him in a crimson curtain.

Only the dark gray of his skin is exposed to the candlelight around us. From where I am standing I can make out the thin, raised scars on his neck. Only a few decorate his face. His massive hands that look like they could span my entire waist also have a smattering of scars and calluses. A face of striking features and a strong jaw sit under long tresses of raven black hair. Eyes of burning, red flames look down at me. Consuming me so completely I can barely breathe.

This is a warrior before me and he is the most terrifyingly beautiful thing I have ever seen.

My mouth is suddenly dry. I open it to speak, to ask where my friend went, but that's when I notice it. The most devastating part of this primal stranger.

The pointed black crown that sits at his brow.

The pointed black crown of Myrkorvin. Of King Arkain of the Dark Elves.

"My king," Wylan booms behind me. I notice many in the room have regained their composure and light and dark elves alike dip into a curtsy. My knees have locked and I am unable to do anything but stare wide-eyed and blink up at him.

"It seems as though you have given Myrkorvin a gift and selected a bride."

Ice freezes my veins. No…it can't be. I was so careful. And Ari, he would not have tricked me, would he? I received no favor and entered into no bargain.

But even as I think it, I realize what has happened. My hand comes up over my mouth and something passes in the king's eyes. Too brief for me to make it out but for a second I could swear it was shame. Those eyes harden as he looks up to the dais.

"It seems as though I have," King Arkain says, in a voice that pours over my body like warm honey. This cannot be happening. My family. My mother. My father. My brother. What will they all think? What will they say?

My knees wobble and my vision goes dark. The last thing I see before it consumes me is Arkain lunging for me with a curse and the feeling of the cool leather of his armor through the thin fabric of my dress.

CHAPTER TEN

ARKAIN

IN HINDSIGHT, THIS WHOLE THING could've gone a bit smoother.

Instead of securing forces through a politically advantageous marriage I have a bride-to-be who fainted at the first sight of me. A very worried Lysan royal family when they heard their only daughter was being taken to see one of my healers. Once they found out they were going to check-in on Myrkorvin's queen-to-be they had turned incredulous.

None more so than Garren. The prick. Who I thought was going to try and strangle me the moment the guards brought us all into my private meeting quarters. I'd love to see him try. To get a chance to repay his cowardice. Future in-laws be damned.

Princess Elveena is currently occupying the next room over. There was so much that happened between her fainting and me being here with her family that I barely got a chance to process the fact that I was holding her in my arms. She's a tiny thing. Lithe, with small curves and delicate features. She weighed absolutely nothing in my arms and I had to suppress a growl when the healers came and took her away.

Which is something I am choosing not to examine too closely. Or the fact that even the blue hue I had her mask enchanted to display so I could easily find her tonight was something I did not need. Pure instinct drew me to find the princess as she emerged outside of the castle.

Due to that, I am taking it as a sign from the free magic and the First Gods that my plan, though deceitful, was necessary and this is their way of blessing it. Or so I hope.

The king and queen of Lysan cut opposing figures. Queen Mirella's

58

face is so much like her daughter's. But where Elveena is playful, Mirella is guarded. Her royal mask in place. As is Orvian's. Their younger son Briar is sitting, fiddling with a loose string on his tunic. He has not said a word since they were informed that Elveena is to be my bride. To be honest, no one in the royal family has really said much.

Except for Garren, who sits simmering with rage in the corner. Even his mate seems unsure what to do. Going from leaning against the wall, to sitting, to standing. I know the silence is making them uncomfortable and truthfully, I should be the one to break it. Wylan had wanted to speak to me before I talked to the Lysan royals but I had been too preoccupied with making sure Elveena was okay.

He was always better at diplomacy than me and now I wish I had made time to hear him out.

"So what does this mean?" King Orvian speaks quietly. "For my daughter? For you? For our kingdoms?"

"The rules of the Night are simple," I find myself saying. My voice sounds sharp even to my own ears. "Your daughter participated. She was chosen and the bargain was struck. She will be my wife and queen of Myrkorvin. The free magic has willed it."

"Free magic?" Garren laughs without humor. "Or one of your foul tricks. This was obviously some sick ploy to get us here. Tell us what you want and hand us back my sister and we will be on our way."

His gold eyes are hard. The face of a proud prince is now twisted into a sneer. Deep inside me, a growl is loosened. I bare my teeth at him and he rears back. I know he's remembering that day. Of what I can do if I do not keep myself in check.

"Watch how you speak to me, *prince*. You do not give me orders."

"Garren," King Orvian says, "if you cannot speak to the king with respect you will be removed from these rooms. I will not have your outbursts harming your sister."

"You are the one who insisted she attend, Father. You sent your precious Elvie here to be a lamb for the slaughter! So do not lecture me on keeping her safe when it is your fault we are in this position in the first place."

"Garren," Queen Mirella says, rising to her feet to stand beside her husband. Her voice is soft but there is no mistaking the warning in it. "Speak again and I will have you removed."

Garren swallows and his mate leads him back to the chair she has vacated for the fifth time. I smirk at that, how quickly he is dismissed by his parents. How the power he has is only his if they allow it.

Not absolute like mine. That makes my smirk deepen as his face turns a disturbing shade of purple.

"King Arkain, I implore you king to king, to break this bargain between you and my daughter. If it is an alliance you want, you have it. But please do not keep her here, she is no more than a child. You know what keeping her here will—"

"You will forgive me, King Orvian, if your promise of alliance does not hold much sway with me. I remember the last dark elf king who thought you could be relied upon." I cut a glare towards Garren, his blunt fingers digging into the dark wood of the chair. "The princess was chosen as my bride. It could've been anyone who participated, but the magic pushed me towards her. How are we to argue with what the gods decide?"

"And how are we to believe that you found my daughter purely through chance and not through deceit?" Mirella asks. I laugh and shake my head. She is astute.

"Are you calling me a liar, queen?"

"I am only trying to see if the male my only daughter is about to be forced to marry is an honest one. As any good mother would."

Forced. That makes my face tighten. That is how they view me. How they've always viewed us. Monsters who steal maidens in the night like the orcs to the east. A beast that will debase their precious daughter. Despite what they think, I'm not that kind of monster.

I would not hurt her. I am more curious about the princess than anything. A feeling that I will be shelving for now while I deal with her family.

"Your daughter will be safe here. As she will be mine and the citizens of Myrkorvin will have no choice but to respect her. The creatures have no choice but to fear her or risk my wrath."

Mine. The word clangs through me and settles the being that lives inside me. Elveena will be mine.

"What is it that you want?" King Orvian snaps. Finally, showing those claws my father always said he was the best at keeping hidden. "Whatever you want you can have it. Just please do not keep my daughter here. Whatever game this is, whatever trick you have orchestrated. End it. She's not meant for a place like this. You know it, I know it. She is young and you will damn her to a loveless union for the rest of her days."

Mirella snaps her head towards her husband, shock written on her face. Even the second son looks up at his father in disbelief. My smile at King Orvian is all teeth.

"You brought your daughter here. If anyone is to blame for her fucking eternity of unhappiness it is you."

King Orvian's royal mask slips and I come face to face with an enraged male. He goes to grab the sword at his hip and I jump to my feet. It has been too long since I have fought a worthy opponent. There are a few tense moments, as the two of us kings decide if this is how we want our legacies to play out. King Orvian a dead king and me a king-killer.

But before they can write stories about our impending fight, the heavy wooden door to the chambers are pushed open. Elveena is awake.

Her mother gasps and rushes to her side. Orvian removes his hand from his sword and follows swiftly after his wife.

"Elvie, you should be resting. It is too soon for you to be walking around," Mirella says, feeling all over her daughter's head. Now that her tiara was removed and her braids taken out the full expanse of her silver hair floats around her. Curling slightly away from her face, she looks pale but her rosy color is slowly returning.

For some reason that makes me happy to see.

Garren rises from his chair and makes for his sister. Elveena cuts him a look as he approaches.

"I've had enough of this. Arkain just tried to murder Father, we are not staying here. Elveena, let's go." I let loose another growl as he attempts to wrap a hand around her upper arm.

At the same time Elveena turns, missing his outstretched hand and pinning him with a glare of her own. She is a fierce little thing. That alone is enough to make my lips lift and into a smile and pride warms my chest.

"No one is going to kill anyone," Elveena says. Her voice is soft, gently caressing my ears. "I would like to speak to King Arkain alone."

My name, my real name out of her mouth is enough to make my knees buckle. I'll be thinking about the way it sounded out of her mouth when I am stroking my cock later, remembering her scent and imagining her saying my name as she's coming.

Over and over again. *Arkain, Arkain, Arkain...*

I'm so lost in my thoughts that I almost don't realize what she has said. Alone, she wants to be alone with me. Elveena's silver eyes are boring into her father's, almost as if silent words are passing between them. Garren looks ready to argue but King Orvian nods.

"We will give them the room." One by one they file out. Before long it is just me and Elveena in this chamber. She is still looking at the door her family just exited. Her thin shoulders begin to shake and my heart twists thinking that she is crying.

I move to comfort her, but what can I say? I was never good for comforting in the first place. In this instance I am the reason for her tears, what can I apologize for? Tricking you? Keeping you? Winning your hand in marriage through a couple of well-placed lies?

I guess all of those would be good things to apologize for.

I almost do it too, but then she turns to me. She is not crying at all but laughing. And she cannot stop. Her shoulders continue to shake as she throws her head back and lets out the most beautiful laugh I've ever heard. She looks me in my eyes and I am at a loss at what to do.

Do I join in? Do I ask her what's so funny? Do I call in the healer to see if maybe her fainting had done some internal damage to her head?

Elveena lifts a delicate hand to her face and wipes away a few stray tears that have leaked from her eyes before collapsing into one of the chairs next to the table. With her long legs straight out in front of her, the sides of her dress open, revealing her bare feet to her upper thighs.

I have to look away and try not to think about her thighs again. Lest she see or scent my hardening cock. She has turned me into no better than the unblooded warrior I used to be.

"I have to say," she says, "I've gotten myself into sticky situations before. But this one." She lets out a breath and laughs again. "This one has got to be the worst."

"A sticky situation is a nice way of putting this, I suppose." I want to slap myself. I was never very good at talking to females but of all the things I could say, that is the first sentence I chose to say to her. I should be reassuring her. Telling her that I will be kind to her and find a way to make her happy.

But I cannot say that. The simple fact is that she may spend the rest of her life miserable in order to secure the alliance I need to keep my kingdom safe.

As if she can read my thoughts, she turns those silver eyes on me again. "Why me?"

I shrug. She does not need to know the lengths to which I went to orchestrate this evening. "It is the will of free magic. I bestowed my favor on you and you accepted it. Quite simple."

"I accepted under false pretenses." I smile at her, but I do not think it is a pleasant one because she raises a pale brow at me.

"You should've known better than to trust anyone on Myrkorvin soil. Dark elves are tricksters. Or did your parents leave you so woefully ignorant of our kind?"

She scoffs at that and crosses her arms. Which does not help me or my hardening cock as the action makes her breasts pillow up, her nipples seeming dangerously close to the neckline of her dress.

"I know more about your kind than you think. And don't insult me." she huffs. "You expect me to believe that out of all the people here tonight, the free magic made you select a bride and it just happened to be the princess of your enemy kingdom? You expect me to believe you didn't know exactly who I was, even with the glamour on?"

She is smart, my little elf. "The gods work in mysterious ways."

"Fuck you," she snaps and rolls her eyes. A laugh escapes me. A true laugh. The sound is rusty, as I could not pinpoint the last time something truly amused me. Not like she does.

"If you aren't going to admit to knowing who I was even with the spell, then can you at least tell me why you pretended to be Ari?" She's waiting for my answer but I will not give it. That particular trick is something I'm not ready to share with her just yet. Or maybe ever.

"You're not ready for that answer yet. But I'll give you a bit of the truth. I did know it was you tonight, there was no version of this evening where you would've left without becoming my bride."

"Charming."

"I try."

"So, again I have to ask, why me? My father would've given you an alliance should you ask for one. You've cut my people off from the ancestral lands. You're more powerful than we are, so why go to all this trouble? It could not have been just to secure me as a bride." She smiles sweetly at me but it does not reach her eyes. "I know my beauty is proclaimed across the lands but I am humble enough to know it is not enough to orchestrate a ruse involving two kingdoms that have been separated for centuries."

Again she is right, but I cannot tell her the truth yet.

"You do not give yourself enough credit, Princess Elveena. Males and men would kill each other to claim you, of that I have no doubt." She rolls her eyes at me again but I do note the color staining her cheeks.

That is when it strikes me that not once has she recoiled from me. Her parents had done a good job of masking it. Garren, less so, even I am not ignorant to the changes in me since I last saw him. The war changed us all and I am no exception. She should be disgusted by me.

But that is not what lingers in her eyes. There is curiosity there but no fear. I thank the gods for this small miracle.

"Call me Elvie. No one calls me Elveena unless it is one of my tutors after I fall asleep during their lectures."

"Elvie." I nod, her name tasting sweeter than any honeyed wine.

"Where do we go from here?"

"What do you mean?"

"Do I go back to Lysan until you are ready to wed? Then once we are wed, do I remain here? Do I go back home?"

Panic shoots through me. Perhaps she is not repulsed by me, but she is already thinking of leaving. Possessiveness takes root in my chest. My father's old words ring in my ear. *To let something go is to lose it forever.*

I know what I have to do even if she hates me for it.

"Come here, Elvie." With a bunched brow, she rises gracefully from the chair and comes to stand in front of me. Once again, I marvel at our differences. How much larger I am than her. I'll have to remember to be careful with her. I hold out my hand and she places her warm palm against it.

Her naked skin against mine is almost enough to have me coming in my pants like a youngling. Somehow I manage to hold it together. Her honeyed scent tickles my nose, as my clawed fingers push into her silky hair. The blossom I put in there earlier has stayed vibrant.

Holding it in my hand, I will my power into it. Whereas hers was light and crisp like spring breeze, mine is dark and cold like a winter's night. The bloom glows quietly before changing into a thin black band. Elvie gasps as we watch it slither down our joined palms and wraps itself like a viper around one of her delicate wrists.

"This is our bargain, Elvie. By the will of the free magic and the First Gods. Forged during the Night of a Hundred Faces, this union was struck. You will remain on Myrkorvin soil from this day until your last day."

She eyes me warily but what's done is done.

I would give anything to be able to keep touching her, but after what I did tonight and what I've just done...I don't deserve the pleasure I feel holding her warm palm in mine. Letting her hand go, I have to tear my eyes away from her wary gaze. I have earned that distrust in her eyes; I have earned worse than it.

Elvie takes a step back from me and holds her wrist, looking down at the band. The contrast against her pale skin seems blasphemous. It serves a purpose and in time so will she. It is best she understands that now.

"Should you try and leave Myrkorvin for any reason this bracelet will bring you straight back to me." She stares up at me, wide-eyed. "You will not be going back to Lysan. Ever."

CHAPTER ELEVEN

ELVIE

THE SUN RISES ON THE horizon, bathing the dark land of Myrkorvin in warm rays of light.

In the bright light of the morning, light and dark elves alike shuffle out of the palace with their heads down, some still in a stupor from last night, others looking anxious to leave. It would seem that last night was a relatively tame affair. And the only elf staying behind this morning is well...me.

Even as I stand atop the stone steps of Blackfire Castle and watch my parents load into our royal carriage, their final pleas for my release ring in my ears.

"King Arkain, let us take her home. There is no need for this," my father had pleaded. One look at the black band around my wrist had silenced him, his face going white. My mother had been quiet with unshed tears in her eyes.

There was nothing more that could be done so I had held them tight this morning before they departed. My father told me how sorry he was over and over again. Even Garren had hugged me before snatching Sybil away and heading to the carriage.

As I disengaged from Briar, this was the first time I've seen his amused eyes devoid of all humor.

"Twenty-eight."

I raised a brow at him.

"I slept with twenty-eight females during the night. Three at the same time. Skeven should triple your gold marks for that." He stops himself. "I'll make sure to tell him what he owes you."

My smile is watery. "Keep it safe for me."

He nods and looks over my head, no doubt at my future husband-to-be. Gritting his teeth, he whispers down to me.

"Maybe if I hadn't been so preoccupied with my own cock you wouldn't be trapped here. If I had looked out for you like Father had told me to then maybe—"

"Briar," I silence him. "What's done is done. There is no point in dwelling on what could've been."

"But aren't you scared?" Briar asks. "The females are one thing, Elvie. But the males, the things I heard last night while I was…" He trails off.

"They're not like us, Elvie. And for a male like Arkain, I can't even imagine what he would be like in a marriage bed. Have you thought about that? What it means to be married to one of them."

"Of course, I've thought about it, Briar." I sigh. I am not as naive as my family would believe. Of course being wed to a dark elf, the king no less, would mean consummating our marriage. Perhaps I would be a bit more apprehensive if I had never been with a male before, but for some reason I do not fear it.

I do not fear Arkain.

For all that he is surly and standoffish, he has given no indication that he is cruel. Bar the whole deceit and essentially kidnapping thing. I know there was a reason for all of this and I am determined to figure out what it is.

"As I see it, Briar, I have two choices. To be afraid of the unknown and live out my life as a kept female, locked in her tower for all of eternity. Or, to embrace this. To try and make the best of this situation." I laugh. "I would rather not bore myself with endless maudlin wailing. Besides, if nothing else, the king will at least make an interesting husband."

Briar grunts and I can see he wants to say more.

There is a part of this that I am leaving out. Something that I do not wish to examine too closely. That last night, when King Arkain held my hand in his was the most aroused I have ever been. The ache between my thighs has not even begun to dissipate.

My lovers in the past had been fun but fleeting. None of them ever held my attention longer than it took me to come. They became too predictable, too eager to please me. Arkain looks anywhere but at me. Yet I can see it in his eyes that there is something he is holding back.

And if I am to be trapped here for all eternity I'll have plenty of time to discover what that look means.

As if my thoughts had summoned him, I feel the king at my back. Like icy fingers drifting down my spine. Briar stiffens in front of me. My brother is no fighter and is half the size of Arkain. It is sweet that he looks like he will try and protect me. Arkain could snap his neck in a matter of moments but the gesture of him looking fierce over me is appreciated.

"Time for farewells have passed," Arkain states. The rough timbre of his voice makes me shiver. "The bridge will only be open for another hour. Get your kind across."

Briar opens his mouth but I grasp his forearm, silencing him.

"Remember my gold marks from Skeven." Briar smiles and leans down to kiss my cheek.

"Take care, dear sister."

He turns from the steps, the morning sun illuminating his golden hair. I watch as he makes his way down to our family's ornate carriage before climbing inside. The door closes with a soft thud and I watch in silence as it rolls down the cobblestone path. Our bannermen on their white Lysan stallions guard the carriage. I stay rooted to my spot until the last of their golden tails is a mere speck in the distance.

I do not realize I am crying until I feel the wetness drip down my neck.

Turning, I face Arkain. He looks down at me with his red eyes, glowing with that inner fire. He should scare me. The scars along his brow indicate that he is a man of violence. His thick arms are crossed over his chest, his fingers tipped in dark claws digging into the soft leather of his armor. Sharply pointed ears stick out from his expanse of long dark hair.

I find myself wishing I could reach out and trace those ears with my finger. My tongue.

Shaking myself, I forget about those thoughts. The last thing I need is him scenting my arousal. Watching as his nostrils flare, I think I have been found out but he merely turns and waves with a large hand.

"Follow me, I'll show you around the castle."

Having no choice but to obey, I lift the skirt of my gown and follow him back inside. In the daylight the palace does not seem so ominous. If anything, it feels a little…sad. My home, Solys Castle, was never this quiet. Nor was it this dark. Back home we had skylights that let in the warm golden rays of the Lysan sun. Here the dark wood of the doors and the black stones of the walls make me feel like I am walking through a cave.

The silence is stifling.

Back home I could never get a moment to myself. There were always servants rushing by to tend to the kitchen or the immense gardens. Whereas now, I can hear myself breathe as I follow behind Arkain. The same plush red carpet I followed outside last night is muted. The portraits that hang in the hall are skewed and caked with dust. These castle servants are severely lacking in their duty.

We pass through another series of great oak doors, all with the Myrkorvin crest etched onto them. Two swords crossed behind a goblet. There is the lingering scent of damp earth as we pass from each room. As if even the air has gone stagnant in the barren halls. I do not get too long to assess my surroundings as I am pushed forward into the throne room.

It looks even more cavernous now that there are no party goers filling up the room. Just a great hall with stone columns in the same black stone the castle is made from. Banners with that same Myrkorvin sigil hang from them and blow gently in the draft from our entrance. Hundreds of candles are lit to illuminate the room. Even with the sun rising, it does not give off the same warmth as the sun back home. It doesn't seem to be nearly as bright either. Whatever magic is at work here, I am beginning to realize the difference in our two lands goes beyond just our kinds.

In the warm glow of the candlelight, King Arkain's throne is easier to see.

There is no doubt that the dark elves are a warrior breed. His throne is forged from black metal that is cut at jagged angles. Rubies of all sizes are embedded into the throne so that it glows like a roaring fire.

We stop in front of it.

"This is my throne room." Gods, if he was any stiffer he would snap in half.

"I can see that."

He grunts and I raise a brow.

"No throne for the queen?" I ask, and he looks down at me. "How primitive."

"Queens have always stood at the side of the king."

I consider this for a second before walking up the steps to the dais.

"I would like a throne. I hate standing for long periods of time."

He splutters, his ruby eyes widening.

"You want a throne?"

"That is what I said." I run my finger along the throne. It is as sharp as broken glass, the rubies cool to the touch.

"No. That is not tradition."

"It's not traditional to take a light elf bride." I look at him over my shoulder. "Are you a king that picks and chooses what rules he wishes to follow as they suit him?"

"Yes." His answer is gruff. I laugh softly at that.

"How wonderful for me."

"Come down from there," he grits out. "You will hurt yourself."

"If you are going to be like this, with all this constant nagging, our marriage is going to feel longer than an eterni—ow!" My finger snags on the corner of the throne. Crimson blood pools from my fingertip. Sucking it into my mouth to relieve the sting, I turn back, bracing to see the self-satisfied smirk on Arkain's face.

I never anticipated almost smacking face first into his massive chest. How did he move so fast? His gray face has paled and his red eyes are wild.

"Are you hurt? I told you that you would injure yourself!" He snaps at me. I wave him off with a hand. Popping my finger out of my mouth, I wave my hand as the skin stitches back together. Wiggling my fingers up at him, I smirk.

"Relax, my king. See? No worse for wear."

He glares down at me and shakes his head, grasping me by the upper arm. While his hold is firm, it is gentle. I get that funny feeling in my stomach again as my heart beats fast. There is something heady about someone who is obviously so powerful handling me like I am made of glass. Not to mention my head doesn't even reach the bottom of his chin.

The funny feeling in my stomach seems to be traveling lower in my body. How odd.

"Come. I will show you to your room where you will not injure yourself further."

We walk down a long corridor in silence before he stops at a pair of great oak doors.

"These are the queen's rooms. Servants will be in to attend to you." I raise a brow and look at the large oak doors. Looking past him, these seem to be the only doors on this wing of the building. How odd.

"Where do you sleep?" He raises a brow at my question.

"The north wing."

"And once we wed, we will share the same room, yes?"

"No," he says bluntly.

"No?"

"No. It is tradition."

"My parents have always shared the same room," I counter.

"Mine were mated and very much in love and yet they still kept their own quarters. Besides," he bites out, "I am sure you would welcome time away from me. A monster has claimed you as his bride, he is not so cruel that he demands you stay with him every night for all of eternity."

I open my mouth to what? Deny it? Tell him not to call himself a monster.

Whatever I was going to say dies as the same white-haired dark elf from last night rounds the corner. Upon seeing me, his eyes narrow. If looks could kill, I'd be already getting prepped for my funeral gown. He bows to Arkain, his white hair falling forward over his decorated black armor.

"Your Majesty, word has come from our scouts in the east. The matter is urgent."

Arkain's mouth sets in a hard line and I see him curl his claws into his palms. The east? What goes on in the east? Then it dawns on me. The orcs. Are they stirring again? I almost ask but Arkain begins to stomp off. He pauses when he is a few feet away and without turning to me calls out.

"We will have dinner in my private quarters tonight. My servants

71

will collect you."

And just like that I am left alone in the hall. The castle is so quiet I can hear my own breathing. With nothing else to do I push open the massive doors and am greeted by the most depressing sight imaginable.

I know the dark elves pride themselves on being wild creatures of the night, but this red and black color scheme is getting ridiculous. The room is spacious but vacant. A large bed sits against the wall with black sheets and quilt. There is a spacious window that is letting in sunlight, illuminating a dark wooden vanity and a black stone tub in the corner.

A royal wardrobe is off to the side. Even from here I can see the different garments. All in the same dark black color. A few have blood-red stitching, but it seems as though dark elves only shop from a small color palette.

With a sigh I lie down on the bed. It is comfy enough. For some odd reason I feel as though I am inhabiting a tomb. There are no personal effects in here. No paints or portraits. As if all traces of the last queen have been wiped clean and the shell of her living quarters remain.

I have to do something to make this space mine, if I am going to be staying here.

An idea strikes me.

There is one place that I did feel more myself and Arkain did not demand that I stay in my room until dinner. Finding a black cloak hanging in the wardrobe, I put it on and exit the room on silent feet. There is one servant who is carrying a stack of plates down the hall. He regards me with curiosity but doesn't say anything. His hair is pulled back from his face in a low bun. A scar runs through one of his red eyes.

I keep going back down the corridor, using memories from last night to carry me. I pass by a few more guards who regard me but then look away. Maybe they think I am not worth the trouble of hassling. That if I am happened upon by a wild beast and eaten then so be it.

The thought makes me shiver but I keep moving until I am out the doors I exited last night. The sun has fully risen now and I make my way down the stone path on bare feet. My toes curl over the cool stones until I find myself passing under the wisteria-covered archway.

There were many tricks Arkain played last night, but I am happy to know that this garden was not one of them. In fact it feels even more magical in the day. While the night-blooming flowers were the draw last night, today there are all types of plants preening under the sun.

Ivy plants and black vines curl up the walls of the garden. Being careful not to trip over fallen branches, I make my way back towards the willow. In the daylight, she seems to be resting. Charging her branches so they are ready to glow when the moon is full.

I am just about to go pick some wildflowers at her base when I hear something.

"Ridiculous! After all of these months he just had to have a party, and now look at them! It's going to take months for me to regrow them!"

I squint as I round the corner and see who is out here.

There, crouched at the base of the tree, is a curvy figure. Wildly curled hair the same shade as the *darksky roses* is pulled back with a leather band. There are countless bags and bottles tied to her sides as she digs through the dirt. Her pale skin is caked with dirt and there is a smattering of it on her freckled nose.

A piece of magenta hair falls in front of her face and she quickly tucks it behind an ear. Which is round. My mouth falls open in shock, before being replaced by a smile.

"A human!" I cry. The figure in front of me screams and drops her glass vial she was putting dirt into. Her round cheeks turn the same shade as her hair as she jumps to her feet.

"Do not sneak up on me!" She shakes a finger at me and I continue to smirk. "I swear all elves should be born with a collar and bell. It is not natural how quietly you move. It is as if the gods made you creatures just to scare the daylights out of me."

"How unpleasant for our females to birth babies with belled collars."

"Oh excellent," the pink-haired human shakes her head. "This one likes to tell jokes."

"I apologize others of my kind were not nearly as entertaining." I smile. "My name is—"

"Princess Elveena, from Lysan. The bride Arkain took from the

Night. I know. The castle has been buzzing with the news."

"Buzzing? That castle is quieter than a graveyard." The pink-haired human laughs.

"Yes, King Arkain keeps the main part of the castle quiet. That's why most of the staff keep to the west wing."

"Right," I say. "And you are?"

The pink-haired human blushes again and does her best attempt at a curtsy .

"Kaethe, royal alchemist. I do apologize, I mainly stick to my lab so my manners when greeting elven nobles may be a bit rusty." She swallows. "Your Majesty."

I laugh and shake my head.

"Don't worry about it and call me Elvie."

"Then call me Kae. I prefer it anyway."

I smile and look down at her. She is half a foot shorter than me. In her linen pants and flowy shirt she is all soft curves and freckled skin. Kae must be around my age. But there is knowledge in her blue eyes that makes her seem older.

"So what is a human doing in Myrkorvin? I thought humans weren't permitted to live here?"

"Who told you that?" Kae asks.

"It is what we are taught in Lysan."

"Well, there are plenty of humans here. I'm sure you'll see them the longer you are here."

"And how did you become the royal alchemist to King Arkain?" Kae freezes and something passes over her features.

"It's a long…story. Quite a boring one I'm afraid." I nod and know when not to pry into something.

"Then perhaps you can tell me what you were doing in the dirt?" Her blue eyes widen as if she just remembered and she drops to her knees again, digging with short, blunt fingers in the soil at the base of the willow.

"Someone during last night's party must've thought it funny to tramp over my *liverworm plants*. These things took months to grow. I've been needing them for a certain antidote I've been working on and this

74

just set me back a few months." She holds up the wilted green leaves towards me. Indeed all the plants near the base of the willow look like they have been squashed under foot.

I put a hand over my mouth. It is quite possible that this was mine and Ari's doing during our dance.

I must fix this.

"Here, let me help you." The free magic zips through me and metal perfumes the air. Kae sucks in a breath as her *liverworm plants* knit back together. The leaves refill and become plump once more. Their deep emerald shade is restored and new mature liverworms also sprout from the soil.

"How did you do that?" she asks incredulously.

"It's my magic. I have a way with plants. Surely someone in Myrkorvin can do the same thing?"

"I've never seen it. That type of magic isn't wielded by the dark elves." The joy on her face is clear until unease clouds her blue eyes. Her face grows serious and cautious.

"What do you want in return for helping me?"

I am confused and then I realize. As a human surrounded by dark elves she is used to having to bargain for assistance. To deal and barter. That all kind deeds are just the means to fulfilling some type of trick.

"I don't want anything from you. Light elves don't deal in trickery." She visibly relaxes at that. "But if you did want to repay my kindness there is something you could do for me."

"What?" she asks.

"You could show me around the castle? I'm afraid Arkain was less than an enthusiastic tour guide." Kae chuckles at that and rises, swiping her dirty palms on her pants.

"Now that I can imagine. Come, let me show you what all this castle has to offer."

The two of us turn and set off back towards the castle. There is a lot that can be said about Myrkorvin, but as I look down at my pink-haired companion, one thing is for certain. Life here will certainly not be boring.

CHAPTER TWELVE

ELVIE

KAETHE GUIDES ME TO A part of the castle I have never seen.

Where the throne room and the queen's rooms are made from the same drab black stone, this wing of the castle is obviously a new addition. The stone is pale gray and there are open-air windows that illuminate the space.

The scent of burning wood and damp earth lingers in the air.

There are also more people here. Humans and dark elves alike.

A human woman passes us, her curly hair pulled back from her sharp face. Paint in all different hues of blue and purple coat her tan skin. Her white smock is covered in the same array of colors. She smiles at Kae as we pass.

"Morning Kaethe, Fredric says the ovens are ready."

"Thank you Breena. This is Princess Elvie, King Arkain's bride-to-be." The girl looks down at her feet and, just like Kae, attempts a curtsy. I am beginning to think most of the humans that live here do not come in contact with elves much.

"Your Majesty," she whispers. I smile and shake my head.

"Please, just, Elvie." I nod to her smock. "Are you a painter?"

"Yes, but I have not mastered it yet."

"She's being modest," Kaethe says. "She creates the most amazing landscapes. Makes you feel like you are actually looking at them and not just paint on a canvas."

"But my portrait work could be better. When are you going to let me paint you, Kae? You keep putting it off." Brenna puts her hands on her hips. Kae ducks her head and looks away.

"You know, I'm not really interested in—"

"Nonsense, you would be perfect! You look just like one of Cheval's models. I've been reading up on his work and his depiction of the female form is second to none."

"Who?" Breena's mouth drops open at Kae's question and I chuckle softly.

"She's right. Cheval would kill to get his hands on you," I say. "He is a master of the art."

"You know Cheval?" Breena says with awe.

I nod. "He came to the palace in Lysan once with a few of his models. The way he paints, you would think he was the one with magic, not us."

"I would love to meet him. Just once."

"Perhaps it can be arranged. He owes me a favor anyhow." I smile at the memory.

"Really? Oh gods, that would be wonderful," Breena sighs. "We never get any visitors here anymore."

"Why's that," I ask.

"Well ever since King Arkain—"

"Breena," Kae cuts in. "We must be going." The two humans share some kind of look before Breena smiles at me and nods.

"Of course. See you around, Elvie."

With that she is gone and Kae continues to lead me down the hall until we push through a pair of wooden doors. What's beyond them is something I have never seen before.

A roaring fire in the back. Tubes of all shapes and sizes take up the entirety of the massive work table. Vials of all sorts of herbs and potions. Jars containing plants and creatures I've never even heard of before.

Bats' wings. Beaverviper skulls. Dwarves's finger bones. Scales from the southern sirens. Jar after jar contains oddity after oddity. Not to mention half of them were illegal to own in Lysan.

Leather-bound books are everywhere. Open to pages with diagrams of all different kinds of creatures. Grimoires filled with different lists on how to create the perfect potions for everlasting life, true love, and everything in between.

"What is this place?" I ask.

Kae looks around and blushes, wringing her hands on the front of her shirt.

"It's my laboratory. Sorry it's in such a state, I have meant to clean up here."

"It is wonderful, Kae."

I mean that too. Our royal alchemist back in Lysan mainly deals with our greenhouse. How to maximize our crop outputs to make our southern region more fruitful. This is a true merging of magic and science.

"When did you start studying alchemy?" I ask. Kae comes to stand next to me as I thumb my way through one of her books. A guide on how venom from the eels of Skull Bay can be used to bring down fevers caused by a poisonous *beaverviper* bite.

"I came to Myrkorvin when I was around twelve. I was able to get in with an older alchemist who thought I showed promise and sponsored me to go to the royal academy. That's where King Arkain found me." She laughs softly. "I was a bit of a rebel, using ingredients even my elven professors wouldn't touch. I guess that made the king think I was perfect for the task he had for me."

"What task?" I ask. Kae swallows and covers her face in her hands.

"I should not have said anything," she mutters. I give her an appraising stare and she sighs. "But I guess if you are to be queen there's no harm in telling you. Come."

Kaethe guides me back towards one of the roaring fires. There are more glass tubes set up with a variety of herbs laid out.

"The king has tasked me with creating an antidote to *orc's teeth arrows*."

I scrunch my nose. "Orcs use their own teeth as arrowheads?"

Kaethe shakes her head. "No, it is just what they call them. They are arrows dipped in a poison made from flowers that only bloom on the Brokenbone Mountains. One hundred percent deadly. Just pricking yourself with one means you will drop dead within moments." Kae sighs. "The orcs have a natural immunity to them but I am certain it is something that we can replicate. Or at the very least find a way to nullify the poison enough to not be deadly."

I am quiet for a moment, considering what she said. "This is quite the task to put you in charge of. What is the importance of these arrows to the king?"

Kaethe contemplates this for a moment and I think she's not going to tell me, but she surprises me and does.

"An *orc's teeth arrow* killed King Arkain's father. The poison is so painful and so fast-acting that you will wish for death. King Arkain has vowed that no elf should fall victim to that same fate." She pauses. "And if the orcs wish to go to war again, then we should be prepared to defeat them."

"Is there a chance of that happening?" I ask, but Kae just shrugs and goes back to the tubes in front of her.

Taking one of the bright green leaves of the *liverworm* she mushes it into a fine paste in a stone bowl. Spreading a thin layer into one of the glass tubes she pours a boiling, dark brown liquid into it that smells of rotting flesh. The mixture bubbles and snaps.

"We all have a small amount of the poison, so I can only keep trying to perfect it so many times…" She trails off as she drops the smallest amount of black goo into the glass container. The liquid hisses for a second and pulses with a glowing white light.

Before the black completely spreads, eroding the mixture and turning the beaker completely back.

"*Fuck*," Kae curses and then covers her mouth. "Sorry, this happens every time. Each time I think I've cracked it, this is what happens. The poison is so strong, I've never seen anything like it."

I place a hand on her shoulder and smile.

"You'll get it, you just have to keep at it." She nods and then smiles as something catches her eyes in the corner.

Walking over to one of the other work tables, she pulls out a green leather-bound book. *Mistress Grisella's Botany for Beginners.* How cute. Kae skims through the pages until her head pops back up.

"Since you're so good with plants would you mind helping me regrow some of the herbs we are low on?" She asks me. "It will be a while before we can get back to the market in Moonbourne and I am dangerously low on *merc weed.*"

"I'd love to."

That is how the rest of our morning and afternoon goes. Kae brings me a plant and using my magic I help regrow it and make new blooms. Over and over again. Back in Lysan using this much magic would cause massive headaches and fatigue. Here, with the richness of the free magic so freely flowing, it is taking me barely a thought to get the plants to grow.

I do not realize how late it has grown until sweat begins to trickle down my brow and two armed palace guards walk into the laboratory.

Two female dark elves are with them. Dark hair pulled back into tight buns. Clawed hands are clasped in front of muted black dresses. They bow and the taller one on the left speaks, her white fangs shining with each word.

"Your Majesty, we have come to collect you and prepare you for dinner with the king."

I nod and wipe my sweaty palms on my cloak. Turning to Kae, I smile.

"I enjoyed today, thank you."

"I did as well," Kae says, a small smile tugging at her lips. I glance down at the table and pick up one of the almost empty jars.

"Tomorrow I'll come back and we can do more *lily of the valley*."

"That sounds like a plan. See you tomorrow."

I nod and follow the two dark elf females out of the lab. It seems that my first full day in Myrkorvin went well. I may have just acquired my first friend, but with each step I take closer to the queen's rooms unease grows in my belly.

A friend was easy enough to make. Now I must see if I can do the same thing with my soon-to-be husband.

CHAPTER THIRTEEN

ARKAIN

IN THE FOUR CENTURIES I have been alive, I have never attended a dinner this unbearably awkward.

We sit in my private dining quarters. A table meant to seat twenty and we are the only ones occupying it at opposite ends. From where I sit I can see her picking absently at her second course.

After an afternoon of training with some of the new recruits, I am ravenous for each course. Devouring heaping plate after plate of stewed and grilled meats. With Elvie being so small in size, I suspect that these massive helpings are too much for her thus why she picks absently at her plate.

We've been sitting in silence since she first walked in here. With a stilted greeting we were immediately seated and the first course was served. That was almost an hour ago and with each ticking second I feel as if someone is placing two hands around my skull and squeezing it. Awkwardness has become our third guest at this dinner.

Is this how we are to spend eternity together? In uncomfortable silence?

I regard her now, staring down at her plate. Her long silver hair is down, a full piece pulled back from her face, showing the graceful slope of her neck. The gown she has on is hideous. The Myrkorvin black leaches the color from her face and makes her look sickly.

"That dress looks hideous," I say and then quickly shut my mouth. What the *fuck* is wrong with me? Why would I say that? Elvie's head snaps up and her mouth falls open.

"An hour of silence and that is the thought you deemed important enough to break it with?" She scoffs. I try to form the words to take it back but she waves her fork at me. "The wardrobe here is bereft of any color besides black. Take it up with the royal dressmakers."

I nod and turn back to my bowl of stew, devouring one of the soft pieces of beef. The spices are strong, just the way I prefer. It is a hearty meal. Honestly, if Elvie is going to withstand the Myrkorvin winter she'll need to get used to eating this type of food. Even if I'm forced to feed her myself.

The thought of that makes my cock harden painfully in my trousers. *Her pink lips open while I stick my...* I cough and clear my head. Those thoughts have no business here.

"Since your version of making conversation is to tell me how hideous you find me," she starts.

"I didn't say you were hideous," I cut in, but she rolls her eyes at me.

"Perhaps we will move to a more neutral conversation. I met someone today." That piques my interest. My guards told me she spent the afternoon in the laboratory so I can only assume it was Kaethe. Unless it was one of the younger alchemists.

Aren't they all men? My spoon creaks in my hand as I feel the metal bending. The beast inside me is snapping its jaws, foaming at the mouth, and demanding we claim her so no other males will get close to her. She is *ours*.

"Who?" I bite out.

"Kaethe. I helped her regrow some of her herbs."

"Just Kaethe?" I say, my temper beginning to cool.

"Yes, she is lovely," Elvie says, twirling her fork. "And a painter named Breena." My beast calms at this and curls back up in my chest. No longer demanding blood from the males who get too close to her.

"How come there are humans in Myrkorvin?"

"Why wouldn't there be?" I ask.

"Because it is dangerous here for them."

"Is that what they teach you in Lysan? That we dark elves drink the blood of humans for sport?" She doesn't get the chance to answer before the servants arrive to deliver the next course. A roasted bird with a side of potatoes mashed with milk and butter. My mouth waters and Elvie covers her hand with a groan.

"Is something wrong? Does our Myrkorvin food not pass your

standards?" That angers me. She is a light elf after all. Even for all her beauty she is still as stuck-up as the rest of her kind. She has to be.

"It's not that. I don't eat meat."

"What?" I'm shocked by this. "Is that why you're so small?"

"No." She laughs and it is the most wonderful sound. "Most light elves don't since they can turn into various animals. We prefer a diet of fruits and vegetables, it's in our nature to want to preserve life in all of its forms."

"Can you change into an animal?" I ask, genuinely curious, but she shakes her head.

"I got close once when I was younger. Tried to turn into one of our royal seagulls. It took three of our skilled court magicians to change me back. I was coughing up feathers for a week." I nod at this and turn back to my plate. Perhaps I should call in the staff and ask them to prepare something else for her.

"Speaking of transforming, is Ari the only other form you use or are there others?"

That draws me up short.

"I can use other forms." She waits for me to elaborate but I do not and she huffs in her chair.

"I still don't understand. Why create a completely false person? You are a king, I am a princess. You could've simply spoken to me and secured this alliance. There was no need to go to all of this trouble."

"Ari is closer to the real me than you may think," I say before I can take it back. trying to divert her away from this new line of questioning.

"How can that be?" she asks, but I ignore her. Talking to females has never been my strong suit.

Talking of any kind really.

"Besides, I could not have simply just 'talked to you' as you so eloquently put it. Our kingdoms have been apart for centuries. Your father, despite what he has said this morning, would not have let me within a hundred feet of you. Let alone hear me if I proposed marriage."

"You don't know that."

"Oh but I do. King Orvian would rather have his kingdom burned than sign over his precious daughter to a monster king. And I needed this

83

alliance," I say.

"Why? You're still not telling me why."

"Why does it matter?" I shout and she cringes and I regret it instantly. Of course she is confused, but I cannot tell her. Not yet. Maybe not ever. "You were chosen during the Night of a Hundred Faces. Your father could have demanded you stay at home in Lysan but he knew that it would be an insult. I knew he would have to bring you and I did what I had to do to make sure you were chosen. Call it deceit, a cruel trick or whatever the fuck you want. But know I would do it again. To keep my kingdom safe, I would do it a hundred times."

"And I am forced to pay this price because I was kind to someone? Because I thought I had found a friend? Who is Ari to you? Who is he?" she asks.

"You're not ready to hear that," I say.

"Stop *fucking* saying that," she yells. "I am so sick and tired of everyone treating me like a child. You picked me to be your wife. I am stuck here forever. I am trying to understand you and why you did it. To make sense of this path I've found myself on."

"A beast does not need a motive to act monstrous."

"Oh gods," she exclaims. "Not this again. The most monstrous thing about you is how you're behaving right now."

"You don't know anything about me or what I am truly like."

"Then help me understand. Tell me why you orchestrated this whole thing just to keep me here." Her silver eyes implore me but my face remains serious.

"No," I say.

"No?"

"You don't need to know why I do the things that I do."

She rises from her chair so fast it clatters to the floor behind her. Placing two palms on either side of the bowl she bares her blunt fangs at me. Her silver eyes are like cold steel as they glare at me.

"If this is how every conversation with you is going to go then we might as well keep away from each other. If you are going to be this obstinate to every attempt I make at trying to form some sort of peace between us, then you can fuck off for all I care."

"No one speaks to me like that," I say. Her disrespect should make me angry with her but I find I am even more curious. I am almost double her size yet there is no fear in her eyes. She challenges me in a way no one has dared to do in almost four hundred years.

noticed, not everyone gets tricked into marriage by an entitled asshole either." Her smile is all teeth. The doors open and the servants come in with another meal. She studies them closely.

"The king will be having the remainder of his dinner alone. Please bring me something that's never had a heartbeat to the queen's rooms. Until the king learns how to have productive dinner conversations, I will be dining alone."

She is a surprise. The light elves I have come into contact with before her were pompous asses, so far up their own with their snobbery it's a wonder they can breathe.

Elvie is nothing like that. She is fierce, my little elf.

I feel something I haven't in a long time. Shame. She is trying to know me and I am shutting her down. Fear is ruling me and that is something I cannot allow. I start to tell her to stay, but she has already moved to the threshold of the door.

Elvie glances over her shoulder and smirks at me. Before I can ask what she is doing, I hear the ripping of fabric and watch in shock as her black gown slides down her slight frame and pools at her feet. She is dressed in nothing more than a white shift, the curves of her ass visible beneath the sheer fabric.

It is through centuries of battle training that I do not come from that sight alone.

My claws embed themselves into the wooden table and I hear the cracking of the wood as it splinters. With a soft laugh she turns and calls back to me.

"Send for my clothes that are back in Lysan. I refuse to look horrendous in Myrkorvin black any longer."

I rub a clawed hand down my face as she walks away, her ass tempting me with each swaying step. She has to know what she is doing to me.

I let out a roar in my chest and send my dinner plate across the room, shattering against the door.

Princess Elveena may just be the death of me. Or worse. The one thing that will make the beast inside of me come out to play.

If that happens, I do not think I'll have the strength to force him back into his cage.

CHAPTER FOURTEEN
ELVIE

IT HAS BEEN A WEEK since that disaster of a dinner.

I have settled into a comfortable routine. I wake up, and eat a breakfast of interesting fruits before dressing in one of my gowns that was delivered and joining Kae in the laboratory. There I help her with all types of experiments and help catalog the vast amount of plants she has in her collection.

Some days we wander the castle grounds. She's shown me the royal library and in the evenings after I have my dinner of cooked root vegetables, I'll make my way down there and find a book to read amongst the towering stacks. Some days Kaethe and I spend sun-up to sundown in the garden. Helping replenish the soils and find new herbs that she needs for her antidote.

Today, we are outside by one of the quarries. Kaethe is listing off the healing properties of the ivy she is cutting, which is growing up one of the sides of the castle walls.

"These are particularly good for settling the stomach and since Roselyn became pregnant she can hardly keep anything down. I'll deliver this to her and then maybe—"

She is cut off by the sound of metal clanking. Distinctly male grunts and groans cut through the air. How long has it been since I've heard those particular sounds?

Too long with how unsatisfied I've felt lately. The last person who I wanted to hear those sounds from, I have not seen nor heard from since that first dinner. It's clear he is avoiding me.

We continue down the path from the quarry and the sounds of males fighting gets louder. It is interesting to me that Arkain has not at least sought me out for that. For all his proclamations of being a beast and his horrible conversation skills, he has behaved with respect towards me. He could've easily overpowered me if that is what he ultimately desired.

Something tells me that it's not. And besides, he could always have a slew of other lovers. He is a king after all. Jealousy curdles my stomach for some unknown reason.

As we round the corner we come face to face with the men training. Arkain is easy to spot. Even among the other warriors he stands out. Shirtless, in low-slung leather pants I've never seen on a male like that. Muscles on top of muscles ripple underneath his gray skin. Pale scars dot his stomach and back as he moves.

He does not possess the grace of light elves but there is beauty in his brutality. He is sparring with two of the other soldiers and they do not stand a chance. With every swing of his sword and block of his shield, those muscles flex, absorbing the impact. Sweat dampens the dark hair at his neck and he fights on.

Maybe he is a monster, but he isn't one that I fear.

I do not know how long I stay rooted to my spot, watching him defeat opponent after opponent, my breaths becoming shallower. That part of me that has always been intrigued by his kind is inflamed by the sheer power of him. Inflamed so much so that I can feel my pussy grow damper with each passing moment.

He is a natural warrior. A king that keeps his kingdom through bloodshed.

My staring must go on too long as Kae nudges me and the trance is broken.

"What?" I ask, and she merely raises her pink brows. I gently shove her shoulder forward and glance back to the sparring pit.

My eyes catch a pair of red ones. Arkain is breathing heavily, his massive chest rising and falling quickly. His eyes look crazed, but I swear I see pleasure in them as well. Like he's missed seeing me.

After being here a week I realize that the emotion I saw on his face is the one I spied on Ari's. Loneliness. Everyone I meet says how much of a good king he is but that he's become removed from them. My lady's maids have told me stories of all the parties his parents used to have and how the castle has grown quiet and cold. And how they not so subtly hope I am the one who changes things back to how they were.

These people do deserve fun. If I'm being honest, this last week has made me feel uncomfortable. We cannot spend our lives avoiding each other. With that in mind I know what I must do.

I break eye contact with him and Kae and I walk back towards the castle. Two guards are positioned out front and I stop before them. Their red eyes look down at me curiously and Kae stops ahead of me no doubt wondering what I'm doing.

"When the king is done training, please inform him that I would like for us to have dinner together this evening." They bow their heads and I catch up with Kaethe.

"What was that about?" Kaethe asks and I shrug. There's a lot of reasons that I need to try to give whatever this is between us another chance.

But instead of listing all of those I say simply, "I have a weakness for sweaty males."

Making my way to Arkain's private dining chamber feels different this time. For one thing, I am not in that horrendous black. Since my own gowns from Lysan have just arrived, I am in a wispy dress of pale blue with sheer sleeves and pearl detailing. Pearls have also been placed in my hair, highlighting its silver tones.

The guards open the doors for me and I find myself face to face with the king. He is standing at the opposite end of the table. He must have just bathed after his training session, because his hair is still wet. He is in a pair of pants and black tunic with red stitching. Red eyes appraise me from head to toe and I spy a little unease in them.

For some reason I curtsy and do my best to seem calm, even though my heart is racing.

"I hope this color pleases you more than the Myrkorvin black," I say. A joke as a type of peace offering, and I pray to the gods he takes it. He's quiet for a moment and then waves his hand, my chair sliding out with invisible hands as I sit at the opposite end of the table.

"You look beautiful," he says quietly. Servants come in and pour our wine and I try to hide the blush in my cheeks. Before I can even take a sip, the first course is served and I prepare myself to be greeted by another seasoned carcass when a plate of carrots and peas is placed in front of me. The garlic and butter they have been cooked in tickles my nose and makes my mouth water.

I notice Arkain has been served the same. That warms something in my chest.

There is a beat of silence and then I say, "Arkain" at the same time he says "Elvie."

We both smile sheepishly and I reach for my wine to take a sip.

"You first," I offer. He grunts and nods, spearing a carrot with a fork.

"I wanted to apologize. For how our last dinner went."

I raise an eyebrow and he continues. "How I spoke to you…I regret that. It's been a long time since I had to take someone else's feelings into consideration. Since I've had to speak to anyone outside of a council meeting. You have every reason to hate me and yet you were trying to understand, but I threw that back in your face. For that I am truly sorry."

Well, what can I say to that? There is tentative hope in his eyes. It is a heady feeling to have this male who is so deadly looking at me like I am a lifeline.

"I forgive you. If my mother heard how I spoke to you I think she would've keeled over. It wasn't very princess-y," I say and he laughs. A real one and it warms my blood. "How about we start over? Try this again?"

"I would like that," Arkain says quickly before biting into one of the carrots. We sit in silence for a few minutes, but it is comfortable unlike last time.

"How often do you train out there?" I ask. He takes a sip of wine and then wipes his mouth with one of the cloth napkins.

"Everyday, I oversee the new recruits' training myself." Of course he does.

"It hardly seems fair to spar with them," I say, polishing off the last of my delicious carrots. "You are so much larger than them."

He chuckles again and says, "I wasn't always this size."

"I should hope not or gods bless your poor mother." I clamp my mouth shut but instead of getting upset he smiles slightly. I press on. "What do you mean you weren't always this size?"

He sighs and leans back in his chair, twisting his wine goblet in his hand.

"I mean that Ari was me." I raise a brow and he continues. "That is how I looked when I was still a young male. I was sickly and small. My parents had been mated for centuries but had had trouble conceiving. A few days after I was born the healers told my mother I was sick. That if I lived to see ten years they should say a prayer to the gods."

"Arkain…" I stop myself, unsure of what to say.

"My mother was fierce and refused to believe their advice. Every day she would pray that I would live. And I did. I kept growing and growing and my tenth birthday came and went. And even as the healers were sure I would lead a normal immortal life, I was to do so in my sickly form. Skinny, weak." He bites off the last part of that statement and takes another gulp of wine.

"Dark elves respect strength. From the first king, we've always had to win our kingdom through blood. A king that cannot defend his throne is not one that will provide security and stability to the realm. So the lords of the kingdom began to whisper that I may not be the true heir to the throne. That this was a sign from the gods that my parents' line was to end with them."

"I'm sure they feel stupid now," I say and he nods his agreement. "So how did you become all of this?"

"Dark elves can mature slower than others. My father sent me to live with the warriors posted in the east; the ones on the frontlines. Then, something inside me unlocked. There was a raid on our camp by some Orcs. We were dangerously outnumbered. And all I could think of was my mother, who prayed for her son to live. I couldn't die at the hands of the enemy without putting up a fight. Something primal unlocked in me

91

that night. And I started to grow. By the time I returned to court there was no question of who the rightful ruler of Myrkorvin would be."

"No, I would say not."

"I vowed to never be weak or scared again," he says. We are silent for a moment as our plates are taken away. Our next course is then served. This time it is a rich vegetable soup with a golden broth and rice. I dip my spoon in and take a sip almost moaning at the flavor.

"Why did you want to dine together?" he asks me. I make a show of swallowing my bite and reaching for my wine as I find an answer. Arkain was honest with me and I can at least be honest with him.

"If this bargain is to stand and we are to be wed, I think we both owe it to each other to give it a fair shot." I look up at him and his scarlet eyes narrow in on me as I press on. "You and I do not know each other. And while our union had an unorthodox beginning, I am not saying we shouldn't at least try and make a go at a real connection. Even if it is nothing more than a friendship, we owe it to each other and the people of this kingdom to at least try to make it work."

He is quiet for a moment and I think he is just going to leave me hanging when he speaks again.

"And how do you suppose we get to know each other?"

"When are we to be wed?" I ask.

"The priests will come on the full moon a month from now to officiate us and proclaim you queen."

"A month, that's plenty of time for us to court each other then."

He coughs and wipes his mouth again.

"You want me to court you? How would we even do that?"

"Like everyone else does. It will be the easiest way for us to get to know each other."

He seems reluctant and then says, "I must confess, I've never courted anyone before."

I raise my brows. "You're over four hundred years old and you've never courted anyone?"

"Well how many males have courted you?" he asks in a put-out tone. I wave him off with a hand.

"I'm twenty-three, Arkain, it's less shocking that I've never courted anyone. I still know how to do it." I purse my lips. "Don't tell me you are still in possession of your virtue too. I simply refuse to believe that."

His face darkens and I take that to mean he's blushing. He grumbles into his wine cup, something I cannot make out.

"What was that, Your Majesty?"

He cuts me a glare and sets his cup down. "I have been with others in the...physical sense."

My mouth pops open in feigned shock. "Scandalous."

"I never had much time for courting. By the time I came back from my time training with the warriors I had a craving for fighting. There was always another battle to fight, a war to wage." They come to clear away our bowls and he laughs darkly. "Besides, you saw me in my other form. Who would've wanted me to fuck them like that? Let alone court them."

There is so much self-hatred in Arkain that it breaks my heart. He wants so badly to be the monster that he pretends to be. I grab my goblet as the servant gets done filling it with wine and a new plate of fresh vegetables is put in front of me.

Looking him in the eye over the lip of my cup, I smile.

"I would've wanted you to, Arkain."

CHAPTER FIFTEEN

ARKAIN

I WOULD'VE WANTED YOU TO, ARKAIN.

That phrase rings in my ears. She cannot have meant it, but there was honesty in her tone. Light elves aren't tricksters, and what motives does she have to lie? This dinner tonight showed me one thing. That Elvie is as complex and interesting as she is beautiful.

A beauty that grows every second I spend looking at her.

She wants to get to know me. To give things between us a shot. This is more than I deserve and more than I could ever hope for. A chance at something real. To give her a good life filled with happiness and companionship. It's what I owe her after stealing her choices from her.

I gaze out of the open window in my study. The moon is high in the sky and it casts the lands into a blue hue.

She wants me to court her. Fuck, how am I supposed to do that? Elvie said it would just be about spending time together and talking. Beyond fighting and fucking there is not much that I can recall passing the time with. The first of which I want Elvie nowhere near. The second... I would give my right hand for just one night with her.

The beast inside me agrees, pushing me to claim her. But I cannot. She will come to me of her own freewill or I will live with this incredible ache for the rest of my life.

As I sit and contemplate what courting her would look like the thought dawns on me.

I almost forgot that it was tonight. Looking at the moon there is still time, if we hurry that is. Grabbing my cloak I exit my room and make the journey to her side of the castle. The halls are silent, guards stiff at their posts.

It isn't long before I find myself outside of Elvie's door. Before I can change my mind I knock.

"Who is it?" she calls.

"It's Arkain. Can I come in? There's something I want to show you."

She hesitates for a second before calling back, "The door's unlocked."

Pushing through, I am struck by how warm her room is. The wonderful floral scent in the air. It's almost enough to distract me before I realize what I am seeing. I scrub a clawed hand down my face.

Elvie is actually trying to kill me.

Her silver hair is piled on top of her head as she sits in the bath. Steam billows over the sides, the water a milky white, while wildflowers of every kind and color float to the surface of the water. Her silver eyes find mine, her grin mischievous.

I will myself to stay calm but my cock is not listening, hardening at the scene before me.

Elvie is mere steps away. Naked and flushed. I must stop breathing. She tilts her head and waits for me to say something. Quickly, remembering my place, I turn around to face her bed.

"You're...naked," I manage to get out though the words sound rough even to me.

"That is how one bathes, Your Majesty."

"And you allowed me in here whilst you're in this...condition?" She laughs softly and gods help me. I hear water sloshing as she rises. I can just picture her smooth skin glistening in the firelight. Her nipples hard and begging for my touch. My mouth. The glorious place between her legs is begging me to...I cough and do my best to subtly readjust myself in my pants.

"For a group of beings who prides themselves on being animals, you all are the most fickle when it comes to nudity." I hear the water slosh as her feet hit the carpet. "I told my lady's maid about our summer festival where we run through the Merrywood naked and she almost fainted." There is rustling behind me and I dare not turn my head.

"I am clothed now, you can stop studying my bedspread." With a deep breath as I try to regain some of my control, I turn back towards her. She is draped in a dark green robe, the material open low enough for me to see the slight swells of her breasts. Her hard nipples push against the fabric and I have to bite down on my tongue to keep from groaning.

"Well, what is it you wish to show me?"

Did I come in here to show her something? I hardly remember with the way her skin is glowing. She looks like a goddess, especially as she unpins her long hair and it falls down her back. Why am I here again? Oh, yes.

Glancing out the window I curse.

"There's something in the garden I thought you might find interesting. If you would allow me to show it to you." I take a deep breath steadying myself. "I think you will like this and I want to show that I'm taking this courting idea to heart."

I peek open one of my eyes at her and there's a soft smile on her lips. Gods, if she could look at me like that every day I would die a happy male. Without another word she tucks her arm into the crook of mine. She is so fragile and the beast inside me is screaming.

Protect, protect, protect.

"I would love to see it, Arkain. Please, lead the way."

I feel like I am floating with her on my arm. The hallways of the castle do not even faze me. Nothing matters but her warmth soaking into my side. The way she brushes against me. Her floral scent that I want imprinted on my skin, my bones, my sheets.

Before I even realize it we are here. The garden. The place where our story started. She must be thinking the same thing as she looks up at me with her cheeks pink.

I lead her past the stream to a pond in the back. The moon is at its peak so it should be starting soon. A gasp escapes her lips as she watches the dark water below. Thousands of small creatures float to the surface of the pond to be powered by the moon. One by one they begin to glow, making the black water look like a star-filled night sky.

"Oh my gods."

"It is only on certain nights, when the moon is bright enough and the night is clear that they will do this." A lump forms in my throat but I swallow it down. "My mother used to take me out here when I was young. She said that a king a long time ago stole a piece of the night sky for his mate because he loved her so much."

Elvie peers up at me with a soft smile as the tightness in my chest grows more intense.

"She would say that love has the power to do anything. My father taught her that, and he made sure that I understood to love something and to let it go was to lose it forever. That is why my mother prayed that I would be saved when so many told her to give up hope on me."

We are quiet for a moment as we watch the fish swim around the pond. Elvie turns next to me and pushes up on her toes. Her soft lips press into my cheek. It is over far too soon and I feel myself craving her closeness again.

"Thank you for showing me this." My face is hot, but I nod. She looks around the garden and then turns back to me.

"Do you have to be king all day tomorrow or can you spare a few hours?"

"I meet with my advisors in the morning but I can cancel everything in the afternoon. Why? Did you have something in mind?"

Her beautiful face morphs into something that is purely dark elf.

"You'll see."

CHAPTER SIXTEEN

ELVIE

ARKAIN'S ADVISORS LOOKED SHOCKED TO see me as they file out of his meeting room.

Most of them give me a wide berth and while I spy disgust in some of their eyes, there are a few who rake me with appreciative stares. Gross. They are all dressed in Myrkorvin black, long red capes trailing behind them. Once again, the difference between our kinds could not be more apparent. But even after a week, the initial shock and curiosity I felt in seeing their faces has dissipated.

The only one I recognize leaving is the one at the end. Wylan's red eyes harden as they see me and he mutters something under his breath that I cannot make out. It's the same anytime I see him. He looks at me as though I am the filth beneath his boot.

I slip into the meeting room and Arkain whirls around, his mouth falling open as he sees me.

"What are you wearing?" he chokes out. I laugh and do a little twirl.

"Come on, don't tell me you've never seen a female in pants before." This pair is one of my favorites from back home. Loose linen pants that stop just at my navel with a matching top ending below my breasts. It is modest except for the strips of my stomach that it shows.

"I've never seen pants like those before." He pushes away from the table and walks over in front of me. Something has changed between us since last night. I know he feels it too. And that knowledge makes me bold.

"For what I have planned I cannot be confined to a dress." I slip my arm through his and try not to snuggle into his warmth. With a sigh, he follows me out of the room muttering something about removing the eyes of every male that has seen me in this outfit. I nudge him with my shoulder as we make our way towards my new favorite spot of the castle.

Our silence is comfortable as we arrive at the library. The librarian is used to seeing me but upon seeing Arkain, the ancient dark elf rises and drops into a bow, black cloak brushing the floor.

"Your Majesty, welcome." Arkain nods and I lead him towards the back. The fire is roaring and the large leather couches are unoccupied. A stack of books I forgot to reshelve are still sitting on one of the end tables.

"I know this isn't a magical fish, but I thought this could be a good way for us to get to know each other."

"A trip to the library?" He raises his brows at me, but I ignore his quip.

"Here's my idea: we could read each other's favorite books. You tell me your three favorites, I'll tell you mine. Then we can have something neutral to talk about during dinner." I try to keep the hopefulness out of my tone. He could very well hate this idea and dismiss me. "What do you say?"

He's quiet for a moment, cupping his chin with his clawed hand. He looks around the library as if he's never seen it before. The silence stretches on and I just have to ask.

"You do have three favorite books, don't you?" He nods his head slowly.

"Sure. *A Formidable Water: A Comprehensive Guide to Sea Battle, Mountain Terrain Battles and How to Win Them,* and *The Complete History of the First War.*" He lists them all off with a tick of his clawed fingers and my mouth pops open. He cannot be serious.

"What?"

"Are all the books you've read war manuals?"

"Yes," he answers, confused. "What else would they be?"

"I don't know, how about anything else? No tales of knight's bravery? Of lost lovers and the poems they have written about them?" He looks at me like I've grown two heads and I sigh. "I am not reading a war book."

"But this was your idea—"

"Well, I changed my mind," I say and walk over to the stack of books I have left there. One catches my eye and I smile. "Here, how about this?"

Arkain takes the small book from my hand and reads the front page. "*The Tears of the Sea?*"

"Don't act too excited."

"What's it about?" he asks, flipping it over to examine the back.

"It's a beautiful story about a human knight and siren that fall in love."

"That's it?" he asks.

"No, that's not it," I grind out. "But if I tell you the rest then I'll be spoiling what happens."

"Very well," he says and tucks the book under his arm. "I'm not sure what I should pick for you to read since you seem so opposed to my reading tastes."

"You'll forgive me if I don't trust your choices when it comes to engaging reads." I snatch the book back from under his arm and move to one of the leather couches. I sink into the cool, deep cushions and pat the space beside me. "My new plan is for us to read this together. One chapter a night after we have dinner. What do you say?"

He walks over to me, his massive frame blocking out the warmth of the fire before he sinks down, causing me to slide toward him on the cushion.

"Sorry," he mutters, but I wave him off. Pressed against him like this, I'm having a hard time not nuzzling into his warmth. And the fact that I'm squeezing my legs together so hard so he does not scent just how much I *like* picturing nuzzling into his side.

Maybe I didn't think this all the way through?

"So, do we have a deal?"

"Do you want to do the reading or shall I?" I contemplate this for a moment before answering.

"We'll switch off. I like the sound of your voice." I look up at him but he can't meet my eyes, the skin under his eyes darkening. "So how about we get in a few chapters now before dinner?"

He nods his head and I open to the first chapter of the book.

"This was a very good courting suggestion," He says before I can begin. Laughing I shake my head.

"Oh Arkain, you haven't seen anything yet. Now hush," I say and lose the battle with trying to remain aloof. I rest my head on his massive shoulder. Pulling my knees up I prop open the book and begin.

"Once upon a time, the last siren princess sang a mournful song…"

CHAPTER SEVENTEEN

ARKAIN

IT HAS NOT BEEN SINCE before my parents passed that I can honestly say I've felt anywhere close to happy.

But these last two weeks have felt like a dream. That is all thanks to Elvie and our courting. Every morning I wake up excited to see what the day will bring. I find myself rushing through training just so I can get ready for my evening with her.

I could not pick a favorite thing that we do together. Perhaps it is those quiet nights after dinner in the library where we read a chapter of our book and she is curled up against my side. Where we tell stories in the dark and try not to laugh too loud and disturb the librarian.

So many times it would've been easy to kiss her. To lean down as she stared up at me with those big silver eyes and took her sweet mouth in mine. I got close once. So desperate for a taste that I swore I'd do it as soon as I finished the chapter. But by the time I did she had fallen asleep against my shoulder, her soft hair tickling my cheek.

I at least got to experience the pleasure of walking her to her room and tucking her into bed. When I saw my copy of *A Formidable Water* open on her bedside table it took all my training as a warrior to hold myself from ravishing her right then and there. .

I will not take what she does not offer; thus if I am to spend the rest of eternity fucking my hand while picturing her lovely face than that is a more than reasonable punishment for what I have done. In those dark moments in my room, I sometimes believe she looks at me with need in her eyes. However, the more rational part of my mind knows it could just be the need for friendship. It cannot be easy for her being the only light elf here. The stares she is constantly receiving. I see them whisper as we walk down the hallway and it makes my blood boil.

Perhaps she does view me as a friend and if that is all I am to her then I will be grateful. But even that still confuses me. The more I think about it, I wonder why she doesn't hate me. Why, even now as we sit in the garden planting *riverhearts* for Kaethe's latest potion in the soft soil of the stream, she is choosing to be in my company.

There is a bit of dirt on her cheek as she wipes at it with the back of her hand. We've been working in silence for a few moments and I know I shouldn't ruin it. But just like with anything concerning Elvie, I cannot help myself.

"Why don't you hate me, Elvie?" I ask the question softly and her hands freeze in the dirt. Silver eyes shoot to mine.

"Why would you ask me that?"

"If I was in your position I would hate me." I try to hold it back but it comes flooding out. "That night when you found out I had taken you through a trick, I would've kicked and screamed and fought. I would've tried to kill me. Had my family try and smuggle me out. Yet, you've stayed and chosen to remain with me."

"Well, I can't leave. Isn't that how the bargain works?" she asks. I nod, shame rendering me mute. "Then I have no choice but to make the best of the situation. Sure, I could've screamed and yelled and tried to kill you, but what good would that have done me?" She wipes her hands on the white smock she is wearing and looks up at me.

"To tell you the truth, Arkain, there isn't much difference between my life here versus my life in Lysan. I am different here, people watch me here, but I have the freedom to do what I want... except leave of course." She smiles softly at that. "I don't know. At least here I get to be a queen. Back home I'd probably be married off to whatever noble didn't mind that I wasn't a virgin. For all our refinery, light elves aren't ones to break with traditions."

She goes deathly still and her face pales.

"Oh gods, you didn't think I was still one, did you? I meant to tell you, closer to our wedding night. Not that I am, of course, obligated to tell you but oh gods, I—"

"Elvie," I grasp her shoulder. "I don't care."

She takes a breath. "You don't?"

"No," I say, and it is the truth. Elvie has a free spirit and I am glad she lived before she met me and I trapped her here.

Well, I can't leave, can I?

Gods, I am a bastard for making her believe that. Turning back to the soil I dig my claws into it, readying it for another seed.

"That isn't to say that the idea of another male touching you is something I ever want to think about." She laughs.

"Believe me, Arkain, none of my lovers were anything like you."

"None of mine were like you either."

Elvie goes to plant another seed just as I do and our hands tangle. I laugh as we both apologize. Her skin is what stops me. Just another reason for me to feel like a complete bastard. Over these past few weeks Elvie's coloring has changed. No longer does she hold that warm golden hue that runs in her family.

Kaethe is the one who noticed it first. Cornered me about it when I had come to check on her progress with the potion.

"She needs Lysan sun."

"Why?" I had asked.

"Because she is sick, Your Majesty. The sun is different there. I read about it in one of my texts. Without getting exposed to it she'll keep getting worse. The free magic has strengthened her magic but our cold sun is making her body weaken."

There is a way I could fix this. Easily. It is a risk and one I'll have to run by Wylan before I decide anything.

Holding the last *riverheart* seed in her hand, she places it in the ground before I cover it with damp soil. The musty earth smell is thick in the air and I wipe my hands on my pants as we both sit and admire our handiwork.

"My brother Briar used to eat so many of these that my mother was convinced he would turn into one." Her lips tip fondly at the memory. Another thing I have noticed over my weeks with Elvie is that when she speaks of her family she has countless stories about all of them. Except for Garren. It's none of my business but I'm greedy. I want to know everything about her that I can.

"You never share any stories about Garren. Were you two not close?"

Elvie sighs and sits back so that she can hug her knees to her chest.

"By the time I was born, Garren was already mated and doing his best to be the perfect 'king in training.' He didn't have time for a sister. I think he always resented how much our father loved me." She sighs. "I mean, you met him. He's so fucking obnoxious he's hard to get along with. I swear Sybil must have done something truly terrible for the gods to match her with him."

I can't help but agree with her.

"I knew him," I say and she turns to look at me. "During the Orc Wars."

"He never talks about it," she says. My laugh is bitter.

"I suppose he wouldn't have much to say seeing as how he was the one who left us to be slaughtered."

"Arkain," she warns, but I press on, unable to stop.

"I know about your kind's rules on killing, but this would've been just. And even if he had turned into one of us he would've been celebrated as a hero. Instead of the coward who deserted us."

"It's not that simple for us. You know that." She scrunches her brow, a confused look marring her features. "And what do you mean if—"

Something catches my eye in the corner. A black viper lunges from the water straight towards Elvie. With a roar I launch myself at her and she screams. Sending out a bolt of my magic, the snake is thrown back into the pond, albeit without its head, before it has the chance to embed its fangs in Elvie.

Elvie.

Who is now pinned beneath me in the damp grass. Her breathing is coming faster and her breasts press into my chest. Up close, those silver eyes are streaked with hues of blue and gold. Mesmerizing. I should get off of her, I must be crushing her. I go to lift myself off but her hands catch my arms, holding me in place.

"You saved me," she whispers, her voice full of wonder. It is the breathy tone that makes my cock harden against her and that little gasp she gives in response breaks me. Embedding my claws in the dirt beside her head. Our foreheads press together, her breath tickling my lips.

But I wait for her to give me a sign. A signal that this is okay with her. When she curls her fists into my tunic and closes her eyes, I say a prayer of thanks to the gods.

That's it. I've waited too long to be denied this.

My lips descend on hers and I am about to taste the sweetest—

Thunderous gallops break the spell. I whirl around ready to attack whoever intrudes on us when I see three horsemen approaching with Wylan leading the charge on a black stallion. With a curse, I disentangle myself from Elvie and help her to her feet, making sure she has sustained no injuries.

"He doesn't like me very much," Elvie whispers, nodding towards Wylan.

"Has he said something to you?" She shakes her head no but that does not stop the unease that spreads in my stomach. I know Wylan was resistant to my plan with Elvie but if he is making her feel uncomfortable...

The horses stop in front of us and the riders dismount. They all bow and I watch the sneer Wylan gives Elvie who, to her credit, does not wilt under his stare. She only steps closer to me as if I can shield her from it. And protect her from it I will.

"Wylan," I say tightly, and his eyes move to me. "To what do we owe this visit?"

"If I could have a word, Your Majesty. Alone." Again he cuts his glare towards Elvie who returns it with a glare of her own. I almost tell him that whatever he has to say to me he can say in front of Elvie but she answers for me instead.

"I'll see you at dinner tonight, Arkain." Elvie pushes onto her toes and kisses my cheek. Her lips are colder than they were when she did that two weeks before. I have to do something. "Thanks for saving me."

I smile at her as she makes her way back towards the castle.

"Leave us," Wylan snaps at the other riders, who retreat to the stream to water the horses. His white hair is pulled back, showing his old face. Gods, he looks worse than before. More miserable than ever. And there is a distinct coldness to him that I cannot remember being there before.

He waits a moment before shaking his head. "You are a fool." His wrinkled face morphs into a sneer. "War with the orcs is happening and we cannot have a king who is more preoccupied with his cock than with battle strategies. If you wish to fuck her, then fuck her and be done with it."

"Watch how you speak about her," I say, my voice cold. "She is to be your queen. You forget your place with me, Wylan. You always have."

"And you forget my place. I advised your parents for centuries. Parents who would be ashamed to see their only son lusting after a light elf of all things, instead of preparing to protect the realm."

"My parents would see Elvie for what she is. Someone who is brave and kind and compassionate."

"Please, if you need to fuck something so bad, I can arrange for Vysha to come. She would be a better consort than that light elf bitch." A snarl rips out of me and my vision goes red. The tight leash I keep around the beast inside me has snapped. I am barely aware that I have Wylan by the throat until I am hoisting him over my head. He claws at my hand to no avail, wheezing at me to let him go.

"If you ever call her that again, I will kill you," I say, my voice no more than a growl. "It is by my father's will that I do not spill your blood here and now." I throw him to the ground as he gasps for breath.

"There are plenty of other advisors that can replace you."

"You'll regret this," Wylan yells. Pushing back strands of his white hair, he mounts his black stallion and gallops away. The moment he is out of sight I realize he is right. I do regret not killing him.

I pace around in the snow. My beast is still demanding blood and I need to calm down. Elvie does not need to see me in this state. I've done such a good job of not showing this side of me, I can't ruin it now.

Laughing tickles my arched ear and I can pick up the voices of the riders.

"Do you think he's fucked her yet?"

"Why else do you think she's still here? He'll marry her and fuck her, until he grows bored. I say he'll send her back to Lysan within a month." Elvie, they're talking about Elvie. Red clouds my vision once more as I make my way towards them. One is pissing at the base of the tree while the other two sit on the grass drinking out of a water skin.

Nameless soldiers who speak about my Elvie in this way.

"Have you seen her? She's so small her cunt has to be the tightest thing. And pink. I fucked a human once who had one of those and let me tell you, there's nothing like it." He zips himself back up into his pants. "Maybe he'll let us all have a turn with her before he sends her back. Show King Orvian how we like to treat his kind."

"Cheers to that," the other two say and I give my beast the release he wants. Bursting to the surface I feel my claws lengthen and my fangs sharpen. This is the form that killed all those on the battlefield that day.

This is the form that will slaughter these soldiers who speak about my Elvie.

"Cheers, indeed," I snarl, finally making my presence known. The three of them spring to their feet. Muttering "my king" and bowing in my presence. The taller of the three and the one who started this disgusting conversation seems to be the leader.

"We weren't serious, Your Majesty. It was just a joke."

"Do I seem to be laughing?"

"No," he swallows, his skin turning a sickly dull gray. Urine permeates the air. Fucking cowards.

"We're sorry, Your Majesty. We'll never speak about her again," the one on the right pleads.

"No," I agree, "you won't be doing much speaking at all."

My meaning dawns on the three of them at the same time and before they have the chance to draw their swords I've already made my move. The first one is easy enough to kill. I strike out with my claws, ripping through bone and muscle until my hands wrap around the organ I am looking for. With a snap and pull I rip his heart from his chest, warm blood coating my hands. He didn't even have the chance to scream.

The next one I wrap my hands around his neck and twist. A sickening snap and his full body weight lets me know he's dead. I bare my fangs and bite into his neck, metallic blood coating my teeth as I gnaw enough to rip his head from his shoulder. It joins his comrade's heart in a discarded pile.

The last one, coward that he is, turns to run. Before he even makes it ten feet I have his spine in my hands, blood staining the grass below. The beast has had his blood and is satisfied. He tucks himself back into me and propels me forward towards the castle so that we may be reunited with our prize.

Elvie.

Two guards round the corner, no doubt hearing the commotion, and stop short when they see that sight I make. Bloodsoaked and panting. My victims' bodies lay spread out on the grass at unnatural angles.

"Let this be a warning," I say to the two guards as I pass. "If I hear even a whisper of anyone speaking of Princess Elveena with even the slightest disrespect, this is the future you can look forward to."

CHAPTER EIGHTEEN

ELVIE

EAVESDROPPING IS NOT THE MOST princess-like behavior, but as I round the corner past the throne room I can't help but stop and listen.

I'd recognize Arkain's deep timbre anywhere. I've become addicted to its sound these past few weeks. Whether it's when he's reading or telling me a story from his past, I love it. Now that voice sounds mad.

"If you are waiting for me to apologize, then you are wasting both our times," I hear Arkain say. I press myself against an alcove so that I am hidden if anyone walks passed, making sure to tuck as much of my purple gown behind the wall as I can.

"It is not what you said to me that I care about. I can handle your beast and his behavior." The second voice is Wylan. Shivers travel down my spine. "What I cannot handle is it not being controlled. I heard what you did to those guards."

Guards? What guards?

"They had it coming. You should've heard what they were saying…" The last word dissolves into a snarl.

"And you should've controlled yourself. You knew the risks of bringing her here. The dark elves would be resistant to accepting her." *It's me they're talking about.* Perhaps I shouldn't be listening to this after all. There is a brief pause before Wylan speaks again. "She should not even be here."

"You think that I don't know that?" Arkain snarls. "You think I don't know she doesn't belong here? That Myrkorvin will never accept her as one of our own."

The breath is knocked from my lungs. I should not be listening to this. I turn from the wall and hurry back down the corridor. My eyes are stinging. Stupid tears. Why am I getting upset?

He's not wrong. I don't belong here. Does he think I don't notice how pale I've gotten? Even though I'm spending more time outside I am still getting paler by the day. Maybe I was wrong to think I could shape my own destiny here. Perhaps I should've fought harder to stay in Lysan. At least I would've had my family. The sun.

Have I just traded one gilded cage for another?

I contemplate not joining Arkain for dinner. That will arouse too much suspicion though, and the last thing I need is the castle getting a whiff of this. If they learn that the king does not want me here that will make me even more of an oddity in their eyes.

Making my way to the private dining quarters, I find myself alone in the room. Helping myself to a glass of wine, time stretches on as I wait for Arkain to appear. Enough time for me to have drunk a second glass.

Finally, he arrives. His red eyes are wild and he looks angry. What right does he have to be angry? All I've done is try and make a life here. With him. And yet it seems as though even he doesn't believe I will ever truly belong here.

Well fuck that and fuck him.

"Apologies for my lateness." I roll my eyes and that stops him as he drops into his chair. "What's wrong?"

"Why do you think something is wrong?"

"Your voice, your tone, that sour look on your face." His eyes widen. "Something's happened. Tell me what it is."

"Who are you to make demands of me?"

"I am your king for one," he says. "I am your friend for another."

I scoff at that. "You are not my friend."

Hurt shutters his red eyes and I almost feel bad for saying that. Almost.

Our first course is served, a steaming pile of roasted tomatoes in a wine sauce. I was starving earlier but now I can't even manage to pick up my fork. Arkain must feel the same because even he ignores his plate.

"Elvie, you don't mean that."

"Yes, I do," I bite out.

"Have I done something…" He trails off. "Is this about what happened in the garden?"

The garden. How could an evening have started off so perfectly now devolve into this? My body was screaming for him to finally kiss me. After weeks of us dancing around each other, he finally stopped handling me with gentle hands. Gods know I would've let him fuck me out there if we hadn't been interrupted, I was so wound up.

Now all I feel is hurt when I look at him.

"This is about you saying I don't belong here!" I shout. He looks confused before realization dawns on him.

"You were listening to my conversation with Wylan?" He asks in disbelief.

"Oh, don't spin this on me. I have done nothing but try and get to know you. Nothing but try and make this work. To try and make this my home only to find out that you don't even want me here." I stand up, my chair clattering to the floor behind me, rounding the table until I am standing next to him. "Why take me then, Arkain? Why pick me if only to wish I wasn't here? I thought we were building something between us over these past few weeks."

I cannot hide the hurt in my voice. How deeply his dismissal of me has wounded me. Arkain rises to his feet and shakes his head at me.

"You don't understand anything," he mutters.

"Then explain it to me, Arkain! Or I swear to the gods, we will spend the rest of our lives as strangers. I cannot keep doing this with you." Something in him snaps. Those ruby eyes glow even brighter. Moving so quickly I don't even register it until he has me pinned to the oak table. His body trapping me to it as the wooden ledge digs into my ass.

"Of course you shouldn't be here," he snarls. The tears I have been trying to hold back bubble over and course down my cheeks. Raising a single, clawed finger he wipes it away.

"You shouldn't be here," he says softly. "You are meant for the sun. Somewhere it is warm and you can run and be free. Somewhere you can be whoever you want, do whatever you want, without someone watching you."

"But I am the bastard keeping you here. The monster who is too selfish to let you go. The one who took you by trick and keeps you here with a lie. I don't deserve your kindness. Your attempts to build a life here. I deserve you to treat me like a beast. To recoil from me, not welcome me in with smiles and kind words." He leans in closer to my face. I can smell his masculine scent. Leather and earth and something spicy. Head tipping back to look into those wild eyes, something dangerous unfurling in my belly. My nipples harden in response to his words.

"But I am a monster, Elvie. You don't belong here, but I am too selfish to let you go. I'll kill anyone who tries to take you from me." His body presses into mine and that's all it takes. I lean back on the table and part my legs. The moment he realizes what's happening is the moment my scent hits him.

His nostrils flare as he realizes just how wet I am.

"I don't want to leave." The truth of those words settles into my bones.

With a broken groan, Arkain is unleashed. Slipping between my open thighs he is everywhere all at once. His hands tangle in my hair pulling my head back and presenting my mouth to him. His gray lips slam onto mine in a bruising kiss.

I've never been kissed like this in my life.

Arkain does not kiss gently. He kisses like the warrior he is. Conquering my mouth over and over again. I moan and he takes the opportunity to plunge his tongue inside. Our tongues tangle and it's a fight I'm all too happy to lose.

His groan in response makes my thighs grow even damper.

"I knew you'd taste sweet," he growls against my mouth.

"Was there ever any doubt?" I choke out as he moves his mouth to my neck. Biting and sucking his way down to my chest, those sharp fangs dragging along my sensitive skin. When he gets to the front of my gown, I gasp as his mouth leaves me. His claws snag in the delicate fabric of my dress before pulling it down until my breasts pop free.

"Perfect," he growls, his claw lightly circling one nipple, while his mouth sucks and bites on my other. It feels amazing, I can't get enough. I want him closer to me. Using my legs to wrap around his waist, I yank him flush to my body. Leaning forward to run my tongue along his pointed ears. He growls against my breast, switching to the other one to give it the same attention.

"Arkain," I moan and he doubles his efforts. Before I can even realize his hand has left my breast, it begins traveling up the outside of my thigh. Dragging the long skirt of my gown up with it. Oh gods, I need him to touch me there. My pussy is begging for his attention. I can feel my moisture leaking out of me and dripping onto the table below.

"Yes," I pant. "Touch me."

"You beg so prettily, my Elvie, how could any male deny when you look at them like that?" Arkain releases my nipple with a pop before returning to my mouth. With both hands free, he drags my gown the rest of the way up to my waist before cupping my swollen flesh. "So wet for me, Elvie. How did a beast like me get such a beautiful elf like you to soak through her gown?"

"It's the claws," I gasp as he runs one of his fingers through my wetness. He chuckles darkly and gently scrapes his claw along my clit. *Oh gods.* Pleasure explodes inside me. My moan is loud enough that the servants outside have to know what's going on.

Might as well give them a good show.

The sight of Arkain between my thighs nearly tips me over the edge. The muscles straining in his neck are in contrast with his cool demeanor. When he leans down to press a light kiss to my lips, the feel of his hard cock pressing into me has me mewling for more.

"What's wrong, little elf?"

"I ache," I whine.

"Where?" he asks teasingly. His claw scrapes along my clit again and my back arches off the table. Over and over again he does it until I am shaking. Only to stop and look into my eyes. "Where do you ache, Elvie?"

"My pussy, godsdammit. Let me fucking come!" I whine. "Please."

Triumph dances in his red eyes as he smirks down at me.

"Why didn't you just say so, little elf?" Without warning he plunges two thick fingers inside of me and my screams echo off the wall. If his fingers are this size...gods help me. But I can't wait to feel the length that was against me moments ago deep inside of me. Stretching me. "Gods, you are so tight."

Arkain continues with his skilled fingers, alternating between fast and slow, twisting them just right until he's hitting this spot inside of me I've never felt before. The sensation is too much and my eyelids begin to close. My thighs wrap around him tighter and begin to shake.

"Oh fuck, Arkain, I'm close. Don't stop, don't stop!" I chant as my moans become incoherent.

"Open your fucking eyes, Elvie. Watch me make you come. See who it is that gives you this pleasure." My eyes fly open as my back arches. Sweat drips down my spine as my muscles seize. Pleasure barrels into me. I've gotten off with lovers in the past but nothing like this. His fingers are brutal between my legs, not stopping for a second as they pump into me over and over again.

Our eyes lock and with one final scrape of his claw on my clit, I'm tossed off the cliff and awash in pleasure. I almost come off the table as I scream his name. My eyes go blind. Warmth spreads from my stomach down to my toes. I feel weightless. The pleasure is so intense, my body shakes with aftershocks.

My vision returns slowly and I see Arkain smiling down at me. With shaking hands, I push myself up onto my elbows and watch as he gently pulls his fingers from my pussy and licks them clean. I shiver at the sight and at his groan of satisfaction.

"Your cunt is even sweeter than your mouth."

I blush and go to reach for the top of his pants. Dinner be damned. Arkain chuckles and stops my progress, gripping my wrists in his strong hands.

"I think we scandalized the servants enough, don't you?"

"But…" I start to whine and try to free myself to get at my prize that is currently pushing at the front of trousers. Using his considerable strength, he pulls me up so I am flush against his chest. I can feel his hardness press against my stomach. *Maybe If I wiggle just right—*

"Behave, naughty elf. This was about me showing you just how much I want you."

"And I loved it, but now I want to show you how much I want you."

"You will." He steps back and helps push my gown back into place.

"I've been dreaming about fucking you for weeks now. And our first time together will not be on this dining table where I can't make you scream the way I want to." Well how can I argue with that? He helps me down and kisses me gently and I can taste myself on his tongue. After making sure I am covered, I walk back to my side of the table on wobbly knees.

Reaching for a sip of my wine I notice Arkain staring at me oddly. "What?"

"You're too far away." He waves a hand and suddenly the table is cut to a fraction of its size. A four-person table instead of twenty. Our knees brush under the table and I smile up at him. "I've been wanting to do that since the first time we had dinner together."

He calls for the servants who come in, only briefly surprised by the smaller table. Or by the overwhelming smell of sex in the air.

"Why didn't you?" I ask.

"I didn't know if you'd want to be that close to me."

"I think it's pretty obvious that I do." Slowly I drag my foot up the inside of his leg before he clamps it shut, trapping my foot between his knees.

"Careful, little elf. You've tempted the beast enough for one night." I stick out my lower lip and Arkain laughs before tucking into his roasted peppers and releasing my foot from between his legs. "I'm taking you somewhere special tomorrow. We'll leave early so be ready."

"Where?"

"It's a surprise, little elf." He reaches over to tuck a strand of my hair behind my ear, gently caressing the point and causing me to shiver. "It's something I think you'll really enjoy."

CHAPTER NINETEEN

ELVIE

"AND YOU STILL CAN'T TELL me where we're going?" I ask, nestled between Arkain's strong thighs.

We are sitting atop one of the massive black stallions all the Myrkorvin's soldiers ride on. I am draped in a long black cloak to shield me against the cold winds as we ride towards Lastlight forest. That, and Arkain's strong chest that I keep snuggling back into.

From the first moment since I was roused by my lady's maid, I keep thinking that what happened at dinner was a dream. That after nights of touching myself to no avail, I conjured up the whole encounter to finally find some release.

As soon as I saw Arkain waiting for me out front and that potent feeling of lust overwhelmed my senses I knew I did not make it up. Which was further solidified when he pressed a soft kiss to my lips before helping me onto the horse and climbing up behind me.

"I told you it's a surprise." He wraps an arm around my waist and pulls me even closer. My back completely flush to his front and that devastating hardness in his pants pressed firmly against my ass. I wiggle back on it just slightly and he hisses. "Naughty."

I laugh as we continue our trot towards the forest. The dark forest looms up ahead. Even the first ray of dawn's light does not penetrate it. A bird squawks overhead causing me to jump.

"Relax," Arkain whispers in my ear. And I turn around to glare at him.

"Easy for you to say. I've read about the creatures that call Lastlight home. They may be scared of you, but me? I am no more than a morning snack."

116

"The only being you should be worried about wanting to eat you is me."

I elbow him in the chest but he only laughs. "That's not funny."

"I'm being serious." His arm tightens around my waist as we pass through the first rows of trees. "I'll protect you, Elvie. Nothing will get you so long as I have you."

The forest is deadly quiet. There is movement in the branches above as leaves rain down on us. I swear I can feel eyes watching us as we pass. Even our horse is wary, nickering and stomping his hooves. Whatever lives here doesn't want us here.

I'm so tense that I barely notice Arkain slipping a hand down the front of my pants. His claws scrape over my sensitive flesh and I bite out a moan.

"What are you—"

"Shhh, I'm helping you relax. Just close your eyes, we'll be out of here soon."

My eyelids flutter shut as his hand continues working between my legs, rubbing me in tight circles. I bite my lip to keep from crying out. I can hear how wet I am as his claws delve deeper into my folds.

"You're so wet, Elvie. Gods, you are such a treat."

I moan and let my head fall back on his shoulder. I feel his dark hair tickle my face as he runs his tongue up the curve of my neck. His fingers move faster and faster until I'm swiveling my hips in time with him. I pump my hips as pleasure courses down my spine and warms my stomach.

So close, so close…My muscles seize and I moan as my climax hits me. The force of it is so strong I almost don't notice the metallic smell of magic but I do. Just in time to open my eyes and see the sight before me.

"Is that a portal?" I ask incredulously. I feel Arkain nod behind me, sucking his claws into his mouth. "I thought all the portals between realms were closed?"

"For a race of beings that pride themselves on being honorable, they sure teach you a lot of lies." He steers us forward towards the portal. It looks like a giant mirror, only that the glass inside it moves like a liquid. Floating and reshaping. Vibrating with a power I've never felt before. This must be ancient.

"Where does this lead?" I turn in the saddle to look up at Arkain who bends down and kisses me.

"You'll see," he says before snapping the reins and sending us galloping through the portal.

My stomach drops and my vision blurs. The metallic tang in the air is so strong it burns my eyes and clogs my lungs. We are falling. The wind is whipping my hair, the only thing anchoring me to the saddle is Arkain, his strong arm is like a vice around my waist.

I am just about to scream when it stops.

Everything is calm. After a few tentative steps, our horse moves forward and I realize we are in another forest. This one is filled with golden trees and birds singing overhead. The scent of marigolds is strong in the air and it dawns on me where we are.

Merrywood forest.

"We're in Lysan," I breathe. "But how?"

We walk a little bit farther as I take it in. In the absence of the free magic my powers have cooled inside me. But the warm sun overhead is warming my bones. I slip off the cloak and turn my face towards it. I hadn't considered before how much I had missed the sun.

"You've given me your trust, Elvie. Now I want to give you mine."

Our horse stops in the middle of a clearing. We are still deep inside Merrywood, deeper than I have ever been, but I'd still recognize this forest anywhere. Arkain gets down first and then grips me by the hips and lowers me to the ground.

I'm smiling but it dims slightly when I see Arkain's serious expression. "What is it?"

"No one but me and Wylan know of this portal's existence. Should you choose to stay, I only ask that you not reveal its location." My mouth falls open. What is he saying?

With a deep breath, he squares his shoulders and I prepare myself for what he is about to say.

"The first thing you ever asked me was why I went to so much trouble to trick you into a marriage with me. The truth is that the orcs are rising in the east again. They will march towards Myrkorvin and our ranks have still not replenished after the last war. I needed to secure Lysan's army, only this time, unlike my father, I did not trust them to keep their word. I needed to find something or someone they would be willing to fight for." He pauses but I urge him to continue.

"So I orchestrated the Night of a Hundred Faces. Made it so that your father would have no choice but to bring you. I had your mask enchanted to give off a hue so I knew it was you once the magic took hold."

"I already know this," I say.

"But what you don't know is that wasn't the only lie I told you. And if we are to be anything, I cannot start it with this lie between us."

"Which is?" My breathing is turning uneven.

"That you were never spelled to stay in Myrkorvin. It was a lie I told you so that I could keep you. This" —he tugs on my wrist, exposing the black band, before snapping his fingers and watching the band crumble to the ground—"won't do anything. Why do you think you're still here and not back in Myrkorvin? It was a scare tactic to keep you in line."

"I don't understand. So then there is no bargain between us?" My chest feels hollow.

"There is. You would still have to marry me, but it does not force you to stay in Myrkorvin."

"So why lie about that? Why keep me there if it was not required?"

"Because I wanted you. From the first moment I saw you I wanted you. When you looked at Ari with compassion in your eyes, I knew I couldn't let you leave. I knew that if I did there would never be a chance for us to become this." He gestures between us. "But I can't keep it going. Not with you so trusting and unaware of what I've done."

"Arkain..." I trail off, unsure of what to say.

"If you wish to return to Solys, head straight through that clearing." He points in front of us. "I will not stop you. You will return to me in a month for our vows but I will not trap you. Marriage to me will at least afford you the freedom to go wherever you choose. Be with whoever you want."

"And if I choose that, what happens to you?"

He lets out a humorless laugh. "I go back to my dark castle and use the memories I have of our time together to warm me for the rest of my days."

My knees feel weak and my mind is swirling. Freedom? To go back

119

home, to stay in the sun forever. I take a step back from him and he flinches like he's been dealt a blow.

What do I gain if I leave? Freedom to live unattached? Isn't that what I've always wanted? To be able to travel and see the world. To be more than a princess or a lord's wife. Arkain is giving me that. A choice.

But if I make that choice, then I lose him.

I look at him now, his gray face shadowed by the bright sun. He looks beautiful out here. The way the sun warms his red eyes. His cloak blows in a gentle breeze. Is freedom worth losing what I could have with him?

Would I ever find that passion from anyone else? The look of true devotion that is written so clearly on his face. Maybe it is twisted of me and I should be angry at his lies. But there is something that warms my stomach over the knowledge that he went to such lengths just to keep me with him.

"What's my second option?" He snaps his head towards me, white fangs glaring in the sun. "You said I had two choices, what is the second one?"

"That we stay here for the day so you can recharge and we head back to Myrkorvin and continue the way we were. Only now you make your choices with me with all of the facts." He laughs and shakes his head. "I can have your clothes sent back later today.

"That would be quite unfortunate as I will need them when we return to Myrkorvin tonight," I say. The breath rifles out of Arkain and he shakes his head.

"What are you saying?"

I take a deep breath. "I'm saying that I am choosing to stay with you. That you bringing me here and telling me the truth shows me enough of the type of male you are to know even with years of freedom, I won't find another like you." I walk towards him and I know he's not breathing. Pushing up on my toes, I pull his face down to meet mine and push my tongue into his mouth. He groans and grips my ass, pulling me tighter against his hardening flesh.

"And this is your choice?" He laughs in disbelief. "To stay with me? Forsaking your home and all that you've ever known?"

"We can be each other's homes." I say and he nods, a smile playing on his lips.

"So if we're gonna spend the whole day here, what did you have in mind?"

Turns out a picnic is what he had in mind.

Pulling a blanket from his saddle bag, he laid it on the grass for us and then proceeded to produce a plethora of various fruits and cheeses. The sun rose higher in the sky and with it I stripped down to my linen pants and flowing top. Even Arkain ditched his cloak and is lying under the sun in a simple undershirt, his gray muscles testing the strength of the thin fabric.

We lounge in the warm silence. My skin and bones are drinking up as much of the sun as I can. As we eat, he promises he'll bring me back here regularly, as soon as my color starts to fade. The longer we sit in silence, the happier I feel about my decision to stay with him.

Now there is only one last thing to do. I smile at the thought, warmth that has nothing to do with the sun spreading down my body.

"Before I forget," Arkain says and rises to his feet. Digging through the other saddle bag, he produces a book. "I thought we could finish it out here."

I rise up onto my elbows and smile at our copy of *The Tears of the Sea*. Remembering the chapter we are about to reach my smile deepens. This will be just the thing I need.

"Can I read it?" I ask, sitting up fully and reaching for the book.

"You don't want me to take my turn?" he asks, plopping down beside me and pulling me back against his chest. I sigh as his sun-warmed skin rubs up against mine.

"This is my favorite part of the book. Please?" I bat my eyelashes at him and he laughs.

"By all means." Tucking myself more firmly into his side, I open up to where we had left off.

"Now you will recall, we left off and the knight and the princess had just escaped from the sea monster's lair–"

"Which seems highly improbable, I still don't understand how he found her even though there were a hundred underwater caves she could've been in."

"He found her through the power of true love, Arkain." He rolls his eyes but nods down at the book.

"It's still a plot hole but carry on."

"Thank you." Clearing my throat, I begin the story where we left off.

"The knight and the siren princess wash up along a distant shore. Weary from their time underwater, the knight is shivering from the cold as the sun dips below the horizon and night settles in. Thinking quickly, the princess knows she must find a way to keep them both warm. Using the last of her magic to give herself human legs, she pulls her knight to the safety of the shore."

"'So cold,' her knight grits out and she soothes him with a song as she removes his waterlogged clothes. 'Hush. my love, we shall be warm soon.' Once her knight is naked, the princess pauses as she admires his form. Ripples of muscles glow under the soft light of the moon. But there is no time to fully appreciate her hero as she removes her own clothes as well and slides her naked flesh along his in the sand."

"Elvie what kind of book—"

"Hush," I say and turn back to the story.

"'My princess, you're...' Her knight trails off, teeth chattering too hard. 'Do not try and speak, my love. Let me warm you,' she says, snuggling in closer to him. Her bare breast push against his chest. Her leg rising to lock over his hip." I lean back farther into Arkain, his breathing becoming ragged. I clench my thighs together as I feel his clawed hand drag up my stomach.

"It is then the young princess feels it. The thing she should fear but has craved since the first moment she saw him. Proud and firm, it stands to greet her. How perfectly it feels nestled against her core. She moans softly, rubbing herself back and forth on it. 'Please,' she chants. 'Please, my love. I need you inside me.' Her knight all too ready to oblige grips his co—"

Before I have a chance to finish the passage, I find myself pinned beneath a hulking male figure. Arkain's eyes are wild as they stare down at me.

"*This* is one of your favorite books?" he asks incredulously.

"I think you can see why, though we haven't even gotten to the good part yet." I smile at him. "Unless of course you would like a more hands-on demonstration."

He is still above me. "Elvie," he whispers but I silence him with a kiss.

"You're so cold, my king," I whisper, reaching down to unlace the front of my top. It falls open revealing my breast; my pale skin glowing in the soft rays of the sun. "Let me warm you."

"Gods spare me," Arkain groans before dipping to attach himself to one of my nipples. I moan as he fervently licks me, his claws pinching my other nipple. I am desperate for more of his skin so I pull at his undershirt. He pulls himself away from my breasts only long enough to toss the shirt aside.

His gray skin is tougher than mine. I run my hands along the corded muscles of his back, my fingers snagging on the raised scars. Gods he is so strong, and he is all mine.

That thought clangs through me, the truth of it settling in my bones. He's mine and I am his. We are all that matters in this moment. My need for him increases as his mouth returns to my neck, biting and sucking my tender flesh.

I need all of him. He must feel the same as I feel his claws shred through my pants, leaving me completely bare to his eyes. With a groan he kisses his way down my body, licking into my navel before continuing downward.

His large hands span both of my thighs and push them up. I'm panting as I watch him stare down at my pussy. Even from here I can see it glistening in the sun. He must notice it too as he licks his lips.

"Look at how wet your pretty pink cunt is for me, Elvie. It knows who it belongs to, doesn't it?"

I nod my head, unable to find the words. I need him to touch me. The lust I feel is choking me and if he doesn't touch my clit soon I am going to explode.

"Say it." His command is simple, the words slightly rasped with a growl.

"It's yours!" I cry out and am rewarded with a firm lick up my center.

"It doesn't matter if I wasn't your first," he growls against me, making my toes curl. "I'm going to be your fucking last."

With that declaration, he attacks me with his teeth. Tongue and fangs work together to drive me higher to my peak. Sucking my clit into his mouth, I feel him push two of those thick fingers inside of me. They move and stretch me and even more pleasure pours into me.

"You're so tight, my little elf. I need to get you ready to take me."

His words make my toes curl. I'm so close, so fucking close to exploding that all it will take is—

Arkain scrapes my clit with his fangs and I explode on his tongue. My body shakes itself through the white-hot release. Seeing Arkain's dark head between my pale thighs is almost enough to set me off again. When those glowing red eyes meet mine I reward him with another rush of my come that he licks up feverishly.

He kisses his way back up my body, only stopping to swirl his tongue around my nipples before returning to my mouth. His kisses are gentle and I feel like I am floating. Adoration shines in his red eyes. It is only when I feel how hard he is against me that I realize I want to make him explode like I just did.

I kiss him one final time before gently pushing him onto his back. He allows me to do so and I stare appreciatively at the way his ab muscles flex as he lies there. Gods he must have muscles packed on top of muscles. Too much of him is still covered.

That simply won't do.

I slide down his body until I get to the laces of his pants. Biting my lip, I look up into his heavy-lidded red eyes.

"Let me please you, my king." He nods his head and helps me by kicking off his boots. Once I have the trousers unlaced, the sight that greets me renders me speechless.

Holy gods.

His cock is massive. From this angle it looks like it could easily be the size of my forearm. A dark gray a few shades darker than his skin, but velvety smooth. Dark veins run along the side of it and my mouth waters. I do not know how that is going to fit inside me but I cannot wait to try.

My thighs clench in anticipation.

"You are truly blessed, my king," I say. "Or I guess maybe I am."

Licking my lips, I can't wait any longer before having a taste. Trying to collect as much saliva as I know it's going to take for a cock this size,

I tuck my hair behind my ear and bend down. My lips barely graze the velvety head when Arkain sits up with a roar.

"What are you doing?" His eyes are wide and I sit back confused. Did I hurt him? I don't think so, but maybe his cock is more sensitive than light elf males or human men.

My concerns are put to rest when he continues.

"You would put your mouth…on my cock?" His eyes are wide and I have to slap a hand over my face to stop the giggles that are bubbling up.

"Don't tell me dark elves don't suck their males off?" I ask, and he solemnly shakes his head. "You ate my pussy like it wasn't your first time. Are you saying that dark elf females are all receiving, no giving?"

"It's not something that I've heard of our kind doing."

I look down at the massive cock still stretched between us. Gripping his base lightly in my hand, I move my fist up and down lightly and he hisses. It isn't long before I'm rewarded by a bead of moisture at the tip. Leaning down I lick it off, smiling at the musky flavor.

Looking back at Arkain, he regards me like he cannot believe I'm real.

"I can't say I blame dark elf females for not wanting to put their mouths around your cocks, if they are even close to the size of yours." I smile before running my tongue up on the veins along his length. "But if I am going to take you, then we need to make this slick. And I never shied away from a challenge."

"Only if you're sure you want to do this."

"If you are to be my last lover then allow me to be the first and only female to have sucked your cock." I do not wait for his reply as I close my lips around the crown of his cock. I barely have any in my mouth and already it is dangerously full.

I work my hand in tandem with my mouth, gripping him tightly so that I can at least be working the expanse that my mouth cannot reach. I do this over and over, each time gradually taking him deeper until he hits the back of my throat. Saliva runs down his shaft and I make a show of licking it up.

His abs flex every time he bumps against the back of my throat. One of his clawed hands comes to rest on my head and I feel him gently urge me to take him deeper. His hips begin to rise to meet my mouth and I'm choking on his cock. My own arousal is leaking down my thighs, preparing me to take his monstrous cock.

Over and over we do this, all the while Arkain curses. Tells me how beautiful I am. How he'll kill anyone who tries to touch me. All the wonderful things any lover would like to hear.

"Elvie, I'm–" He cuts himself on a groan as I take him as far down my throat as I can manage. I'm waiting for his taste to explode on my tongue so I can swallow him down when all of a sudden I am being hauled off of his magnificent cock and pinned to the blanket.

Arkain is wild above me, eyes searching mine.

"I didn't hurt you, did I?"

"No, you didn't hurt me," I laugh, running my hands up his muscled back.

"You are just so small, I worry I was being too rough. It just felt so good, I almost lost control."

"You didn't want to come in my mouth?" I ask, and he stares down at me with a shocked expression. Maybe it wasn't something he was aware he was allowed to do?

"No, my seed has to be spilled inside you," He says. I huff out a laugh but he seems deadly serious.

"Is that so?"

"Yes, it's the only way I can finish. It's the only way dark elves can finish." Now I am the one who looks incredulous.

"Well, good thing I've been taking the contraceptive tea since I was sixteen." I run my hands down his back before digging my nails into the hard slabs of his muscled ass. "Now will you please fuck me?"

Arkain laughs and his mouth captures mine in a brutal kiss.

"That's something you'll never have to ask for again."

Gripping himself with one hand he's so much taller than me I find myself pushing up on my heels to make sure we can fit together. My heart begins to race as he runs his cock up the length of my pussy. I can see my wetness coating him. Hear the way his cock glides through my folds.

I'm already dangerously close to coming again.

My belly tightens in anticipation as the head of his cock pushes into my opening. My breath catches and my toes curl. Gods, he's huge.

"Go slow," I say, but moan as he feeds me another few inches.

"You can take it." My breath is coming in small gasps. "Gods you squeeze me so tight, my little elf." I see the way he's holding himself so stiffly. Sweat beads on his brow. Truthfully I have no choice but to put us both out of our misery. His arms are flexing on either side of my head and I reach and haul him the rest of the way into me.

There is pain—with a cock his size how could there not be? But there is also an unreal amount of pure bliss. The knowledge that the King of Myrkorvin is fully inside of me makes the pain begin to subside even quicker.

"Elvie, Elvie," Arkain chants over and over. "Are you alright?"

"I'm fine," I tell him, catching my breath. After another moment of stillness, the pain is gone. My body is working overtime to accommodate him and I can feel my arousal dripping out of me. "You can move."

He hesitates before gently retreating his hips and then pushing back into me slowly. Oh that simply will not do.

"Harder."

"Elvie—" He groans as I move my hips up to capture his next thrust.

"Make me scream like you promised yesterday."

I watch the last of his restraint disintegrate. Picking up both of my thighs in his clawed hand,s he pushes them up and pins them to my chest. The breath is knocked out of me as he plunges in and out of me. His gray cock darkens as it gets coated in my wetness. Dark gray disappearing into my pink flesh.

He does make good on his promise and I scream. Loud enough to send a few seagulls scattering out of the trees above. This sends my beast over the edge.

Arkain quickens his pace and I hear our flesh slapping together as it echoes off the forest around us. He is brutal, and he doesn't stop. In and out and over and over he slams his cock into me. The pleasure is almost painful as each thrust steals the breath from my lungs.

"Males would kill for a chance at a cunt like this," Arkain pants. "And I'll kill any male that even thinks about getting close enough to smell you."

"Oh gods."

"You're mine," He growls. "Your heart, your body, this perfect cunt. All of you belongs to me." He pulls out of me only to spin me around so that I am on all fours. Arching my back and thrusting my ass higher, I feel him push into me from behind.

"And soon I'll watch my seed drip out of this pink cunt and you'll carry my scent. You'll give me children, Elvie, a dozen of them. Strong males and females that will be just as perfect as you are."

"Arkain," I moan. At this angle the pleasure is almost painful. It cranks tighter and tighter in my belly. Looking over my shoulder, Arkain has become a primal male, rutting into me like the beast he believes himself to be.

It tips me over the edge but I do not want to plummet down it alone. Reaching back, I grasp his hand and pull him on top of me. I feel his muscular stomach flex along the length of my spine as his rhythm becomes more and more frenzied.

"Come inside me, Arkain," I pant, pleasure coursing through my veins. "I need to feel your seed leaking out of me. Make it known who I belong to. Make it so no one ever doubts it."

He growls in my ear and doubles his efforts, slamming into me over and over again. His other hand snakes down between us and his claws massage my clit and I am done for. My scream gets caught in my throat as I feel my pussy clamp down on him.

Arkain gives a roar that shakes the trees around us before I feel hot rope after rope of his seed fill me. He buries his teeth in my shoulder and shakes with the force of his release.

I open my mouth to say something, anything, but no words are needed right now. Pulling out of me gently, I hiss at the loss of connection. Arkain tucks me into his side, my head snug under his chin as I feel our mingling releases pool on my thighs.

"That was…" I start to say. "It's never been like that for me."

He is quiet for a moment and then wraps his arms tighter around me.

"It's never been like that for me either."

My eyes grow heavy, and underneath the warm sun of Lysan, I fall asleep wrapped in the arms of my dark elf king.

CHAPTER TWENTY
ELVIE

IT IS LATE BY THE time we return to Blackfire Castle.

After dozing in the sun, I awoke to Arkain covering me in his cloak and lifting me onto the saddle with him. The sun had fully set and he said it would be best to get back now before the creatures in Lastlight woke for their nightly hunts.

He didn't have to tell me twice.

I barely even stirred as we crossed back into Myrkorvin through the portal. My bones feel like jelly after the time spent on horseback…and riding other things. I smile at the thought.

Is it wrong that I already crave him again?

Sex with Arkain has lit a fire within me, one that I can't see being snuffed out. Even now as we approach the castle I am thinking if there is enough time for me to unlace his pants and ride his cock before we make it to the stables.

"What are you thinking about?" he whispers in my ear and I shiver. He no doubt smelled the change in my scent.

"If there's enough time for me to fuck you before someone spots us," I say, and I feel him laugh behind me.

"I wouldn't be opposed to having you in my bed every night," He says and I smile at that.

"That can be arranged, my king."

As we approach the stable, I notice two guards are waiting there for us. Arkain jumps down first like he did before and then gently sets me on my feet. The faces of the guards are grim.

"What has happened?" Arkain asks as the guards bow.

"A messenger from the east has arrived. He says there is an urgent matter he needs to discuss with you." I feel Arkain stiffen behind me and he nods before dismissing the guards.

"I'm going to stay out here for a bit," I say, stroking the mane of the black stallion. "I should like to feed our companion a few apples for how bravely and safely he got us to our destination."

Arkain nods, his mind obviously on the messenger that waits for him. I pull him down to meet my mouth. "Go see what the messenger wants, I'll join you in your room tonight."

He smiles at that and with a peck to my forehead, he turns and walks up the path towards the castle.

I continue to comb out the tangles in the stallion's mane when I hear the sound of approaching footsteps. I turn to face the open stables only to be met with the harsh glare of Wylan. Great. Nothing could ruin a post-orgasm high like that miserable elf.

"You shouldn't be out here," he says, mincing no words.

"And yet, here I am."

He scoffs and shakes his head. "You know I'll never respect you. Nor will our people." He takes a step closer to me and I tentatively back up. There's something off about him. He's always been cold to me but this look is more unhinged. "I know how deceptive you light elves can be. I will not allow you to further corrupt our king."

"I could care less what you think of me," I say, backing up even further and looking for anything I might use to defend myself. "Arkain's opinion is the only one that matters to me."

He laughs at that and shakes his head. "Wait until you aren't so interesting anymore. From your scent alone I can tell our king has finally sampled what you have to offer. His interest in you will wane within a week."

His interest in you will wane within a week.

Wylan's words ring in my ear as I sit at Arkain's vanity. I am sitting in one of my sheer robes, combing out the tangles in my hair from riding.

His room is much larger than mine. With a hearth and a roaring fire, a bed that could easily sleep ten. A room fit for a king. There are very few personal items on display. Only an old portrait of his parents and a map of Myrkorvin. If I am going to be sharing this space, that will have to change.

And despite Wylan's words, I will be a permanent fixture here.

I smile, remembering that I had walked into a whole host of servants moving my things from the queen's rooms to here at Arkain's orders. Wylan's threat of being temporary loses some of its effect as I watch the last servant hang one of my evening gowns in the royal wardrobe before bidding me a good night.

A few minutes later the great oak door swings open and a disheveled Arkain comes in. I turn in my chair to face him. He pauses, looking at the wardrobe that is bursting with all of my clothes.

"I see they were able to bring all of your things here." I nod and he comes to stand next to me. "I like seeing you here."

"If I had known how big your bed was, I would've been trying to get in here from the start." He chuckles at that before taking the comb from my hand and gently brushing out my hair. I sigh and lean back in the chair. This feels almost as good as when he was inside of me. *Almost.*

I do not want to ruin this moment, but after a day filled with so much truth, I cannot bear keeping anything from him.

"Wylan cornered me in the stables," I say, and Arkain freezes mid-brush.

"What did he say to you?" His voice is like chipped ice.

"Just that no one here will respect me, that I am only a passing fancy of yours, and that I will not be successful in corrupting you." I shrug. "Beyond that, he was his normal, miserable self."

"He should know better than to speak to you like that. I'll deal with him." He pauses and resumes untangling my hair. "I've never shared a room with a female before. Never let one into this room before, for that matter. To say that you are nothing more than—"

"Arkain, I know how you feel about me," I interrupt, extremely pleased at knowing I am the only female who's ever been in here. "As for Wylan, he was just trying to scare me. Which I hate to admit, but being alone out there in nothing more than a cloak, it did work."

Gritting his teeth, he sets the comb down and crosses over to the desk in the corner. Pulling out one of the drawers he rummages around before pulling something slender out. Walking back over to me, he places the object in my hand.

"What is this?"

"A knife. Have you ever used one before?" I shake my head and he takes my arm, turning us so that my back is pressed against his front as we stare at ourselves in the large mirror. He takes my hand and moves my thumb until I feel a small button. Pressing it, the blade swings out and glints in the candlelight.

"This is small enough you can slip it in your shoe or keep it in your pocket. I want you to have it on you if I am not around. Promise me."

I gulp but say, "I promise."

"Now I'll show you how to use it. Grip it tightly and then punch your hand forward. You want to strike, not slash." Guiding my hand with his, he practices with me over and over. I thrust my arm out fifty times, each one earning his praise. Once I have done it to his liking he closes the knife and sets it down on the vanity.

"But Arkain, you know I cannot kill someone," I say. To care for a dark elf is one thing…to become one is something I do not think I'll ever be able to do.

"A stab with this shouldn't prove fatal unless you get them right through the heart." He grins at me, showing those sharp fangs. "I'll kill anyone who thinks of touching you, Elvie."

That sends a hot shiver down my spine while moisture pools between my legs. It should be abhorrent to me, but I have to admit Arkain's willingness to kill for me is quite arousing.

Arkain goes to undress and I slip off my sheer robe, leaving me naked and glowing in the firelight. Crawling onto the bed on all fours, the black satin sheets are cool against my naked skin. Arkain reemerges a few moments later dressed only in a pair of loose pants. His muscular torso is on full display, with a few raised white scars along his ribs and chest. My warrior king. My monster.

I smile and wink at him before rolling onto my back.

"What are you doing?" His voice is like gravel, arousal turning his masculine scent even spicier.

I drop my knees and spread my legs so that he can see all of me. From the foot of the bed, his eyes narrow in on my pussy. From his spot he should be able to see how wet I am. Not to mention scent it.

"Are you not sore?"

I smile and shake my head, motioning for him to crawl up the bed. Once he does and is looming above me I wind my arms around his neck. My blunt fingers tangle in his long length of black hair. It shifts through my fingers like black silk.

My legs come around his waist and using all of my strength and the element of surprise I roll us until Arkain is the one on his back. He gives a short laugh before it breaks off in a groan as I reach back to free him from his pants.

"I want to be on top this time," I say, finally freeing him and shuffling back to straddle his thighs, before taking him into my hand.

"Anything you want, my little elf."

"Hmmm," I moan, rising up on my knees and positioning the head of his hard cock at my entrance. "This is all I want right now.."

I drag him through my wet folds over and over again. Slipping him barely inside of me and then pulling him out. His groans and growls only encourage me to keep playing. I go to put him inside me again when his clawed hand snags me at my waist, stilling any of my movements.

"Why do you torture me, Elvie?" His red eyes are glowing with lust. Wild and unfocused. His grip tightens on my waist and I know he's about to flip me on my back.

That won't do. I was serious about being on top.

"This is just my way of corrupting you further." Before he has a chance to respond, I drop my hips, sheathing him completely inside of me. His growl rattles the map on the wall. His claws circle around my nipple, his eyes growing even more unfocused. And then I begin to move.

CHAPTER TWENTY-ONE
ARKAIN

RETURNING TO MY CHAMBERS AFTER a morning training session to find a naked Elvie asleep in my bed is something I could get used to.

Her silver hair is fanned out on one of my pillows, her body still curled toward my side of the bed. Exactly as I left her a few hours ago. The Lysan sun has restored her glow. That and the countless orgasms I've given her.

The fact that she has chosen to stay here with me...I say another prayer to the gods. It was a risk telling her the truth. But keeping her here, knowing that whatever feelings she may grow to have for me were built on a lie was something even I couldn't stomach.

I trust her. I can't believe it, but it's true. Perhaps we have a real chance at something.

She twitches in her sleep and I don't want to miss this opportunity. I change out of my sweaty clothes and washing as quickly as I can. As I slip back into bed beside her, she lets out a soft moan and rolls to her other side, the soft curve of her ass pressing against my cock.

I smile and curl myself around her, molding her spine to my front.

"I don't have to be king for another hour this morning," I whisper, before kissing the delicate point of her ear. She peeks open one sleepy, silver eye and smiles, stretching her arms out in front of her.

"Really?" She hums in her throat. "What a lucky day for me." I bury my face in her neck and inhale her floral scent. Gripping my cock and gently lifting one of her legs, I drag myself through her wetness.

"Already wet and waiting for me, little elf?" I whisper and she nods enthusiastically. We groan as I push myself all the way inside of her. The

134

perfect tightness of her cunt grips me like a fist. I roll my hips forward in a shallow thrusts. Her fingers dig into the sheets as I slip a hand around her to play with her nipples.

Her moans are the sweetest sound. I groan in time with her as I continue to punch my hips forward. "Gods, you're perfect."

"I was made for you," She says, biting softly on her pillow. I freeze and she huffs, pushing back against me to try and get some friction.

"Say that again," I demand. She remains quiet, trying to pump her hips to no avail. I grip her ass to still her. "Say it again."

"Make me," she challenges and I am all too happy to oblige. Pulling out of her, I roll her onto her back, gripping both her delicate wrists in one of my clawed hands and circling her throat with my other. My touch is light but she knows she's not going anywhere.

"Say it again." As I begin to move setting a furious pace that she matches, raising her hips to meet mine. The sound of our flesh slapping together drives me wild.

"I was made for you!" she cries and I feel her cunt start to tighten. She's close. Good.

I fuck her mercilessly, the headboard slaps against the wall in time with my thrusts. Pleasure zips down my spine and tingles at the base. I'm close and I want her to come with me. I let go of her throat to use a claw to circle her clit and that does it. Her cunt clamps down on me so tightly as she screams my name. I pour my seed into her, continuing to fuck it into her. So much comes out that it squelches between us and soaks the sheets below.

I pull out of her gently and retreat to the bathroom to grab a damp cloth to clean up between her legs. She sighs at the warmth and I kiss the inside of both of her knees before tossing the cloth aside and gathering her to my side.

"Did you mean what you said?" I whisper as she burrows down into my chest.

"Which time?" she asks before a yawn sneaks up on her.

"The part about being made for me." I try not to let my optimism seep into my tone. Plenty of things are said at the height of pleasure. I would not fault her if she didn't mean it.

"It would certainly seem that way, wouldn't you say? Even now,

CHARLOTTE SWAN

knowing I'll barely be able to walk when I rise from this bed, I want you again." She giggles. "The gods are laughing themselves silly giving me a lover with a cock your size."

I grow quiet.

"Is that all we are? Lovers?" She goes quiet and I think she may have fallen asleep but then she answers.

"Well, soon we will be husband and wife. Why? Is there something wrong with being my lover?" Her snippy tone makes me smile and pull her closer to me.

"Of course not, I just wonder if there could be more."

"Like mates?" I still at the mention of that word. It's not possible, and yet...

"Arkain..." She turns in my arms and grips my chin so I am forced to look at her.

"Don't you wonder who your mate is? If he's out there searching for you?" The thought of another male having a claim on her, desiring what is mine makes my beast bares his teeth at the idea. She is ours, soon she will carry our scent, bear our children...I shake myself from that dangerous line of thought.

"It's different for light elves. My parents were never mated and I've never seen two elves more in love." She sighs again, resting her head on my chest. "And you? By being with me are you worried you're forsaking your own mate?"

"No, I think—"

There's a furious pounding on my door. A warning growl leaves me but Elvie swats at my chest.

"Your Majesty, sorry for the disturbance but there is a pressing issue that requires you immediately."

"So much for an hour before you had to be king," Elvie giggles and I smack her ass before moving to dress. Once I'm in my courtly attire, I lean down to kiss her and tell her to take it easy today before exiting my chambers.

Seeing the guard who summoned me wipes the smile off my face. Especially when I see the royal jeweler holding my crown.

"What's going on?" I ask, taking my crown, already feeling the metal dig into my temples.

"Your Majesty, a light elf is here and he demands an audience with

136

you immediately."

"And who is this light elf to think he can make any demands of me? Much less enter my kingdom uninvited."

"He wouldn't say sir," the guard states as we march towards the throne room. "He said he would not leave until he spoke to you directly."

The throne room is empty as I take my seat up on the throne.

"Where is this guest?" I ask.

"Being held in the meeting room, sir."

"Well bring him in," I say. "He will pay for interrupting my morning." My beast agrees. If not for this intrusion I could've had Elvie at least one more time. At least licked her sweet pussy before I had to meet with my council this morning.

The guards nod and depart to retrieve our visitor. It is not long before two lean blonde male light elves are put in front of me, both of them with matching gold eyes. They could be brothers, but then all light elves look the same to me.

Except Elvie. She is pure perfection.

"I hear you have demands you wish to make," I say. The one on the left steps forward. His tunic and pants are adorned with golden thread and jewels. He is clearly some sort of noble's son. There is a bag slung across his chest. He is probably large by light elf standard but to me he would barely reach my chin.

"Where is she? Where are you keeping her?" he shouts. The hair on the back of my neck stands up, the beast inside me rising again, ready to strike. My claws elongate and I bare my fangs.

"Where is who?" I ask darkly. Both light elves at least have enough wisdom to flinch at my tone. But still the one on the left speaks up, looking at me with disgust on his face.

"Princess Elveena. Where are you keeping her? I demand you release her at once."

"And who are you to make demands of me? Especially regarding the princess," I boom, rising from my throne. He sneers at me with his golden eyes, lips curling up in a snarl.

"Because she is my betrothed and I have come to collect her."

CHAPTER TWENTY-TWO

ELVIE

EVERYTHING ABOUT THIS MORNING WOULD'VE been perfect if not for the incessant banging on the king's door.

"Go away," I huff, and bury my head under one of the overstuffed pillows. It is to no avail as the knocking continues.

"Your Majesty, the king is requesting your presence in the throne room at once. Do you need assistance dressing?" I sigh and sit up, wincing at the ache between my thighs. This is going to be fun. Arkain was the one who told me to relax and now he is summoning me to the throne room?

Something must have happened. I dismiss the guards and tell them I will be along shortly. Washing quickly and slipping on a pale pink gown, I make my way down the hallway, trying my best not to limp. I'll have to see what pain-relieving herbs Kae has. I'll mix them in with my contraceptive tea I need to drink this morning.

That brings a smile to my face. Even though it is harder for elves to conceive than humans, the number of times Arkain has come inside me over the past few hours has put that to the test. The thought of that warms me. A child between me and Arkain. What would such a thing even look like?

I am still smiling as I enter the throne room, but it is quickly wiped away when I notice Arkain's furious eyes from where he stands on the dais. Even with his anger, I am struck by how handsome he looks with his crown. How powerful and dangerous. I am confused until I hear my name called by a voice I'd recognize anywhere.

"Elveena, thank the gods you are alive."

My skin crawls and I recoil at the sound. Ryvik. He is walking

138

closer to me with an outstretched hand. If he touches me I'll scream. Not even the fine clothes he wears can hide what he is. A snake. A true beast.

Trian follows behind him. Always the loyal dog.

"What are you doing here, Ryvik?" I ask, trying to keep my voice even.

"I've come to rescue you, to take you back to Lysan." I back up until I am almost pressed against the wall. My hands are shaking. No, this cannot be happening. Arkain wouldn't allow this. I glance up to the dais and see that he is gone. My stomach plummets.

He's left me, he's going to let them take me…

I feel him at my back. The king steps between me and Ryvik and I almost sag with relief.

"This male claims that you are his betrothed. And if that is the case, your participation in the Night of a Hundred Faces cannot be counted as you were already spoken for." His red eyes bore into mine. "Is this the truth, Elvie?"

He sounds wounded and it takes me a moment to realize why. Arkain, who believes himself so unworthy, thinks I've only stayed with him as a way to avoid Ryvik. I won't stand him thinking like that.

"My parents dissolved the betrothal to Ryvik years ago. He is lying." Arkain nods but his face still remains guarded. He turns, blocking me completely from Ryvik's view.

"There is your answer, now get the fuck out of my kingdom while I still allow you to breathe."

"I'll duel you for her," Ryvik counters and I can't help but scoff.

"He'll kill you within a second." Ryvik's eyes find mine even after Arkain lets loose a warning growl.

"You cannot wish to remain here, Elvie. Not with their kind. Let me take you home before Myrkorvin sullies you further." Ryvik tries to make a grab for me but Arkain stops him.

He'll protect me. Of course he will. He said as much over and over while being buried inside me. With that knowledge, I laugh under my breath.

Ryvik narrows his eyes at me before grinding out. "Come back home with me and we can be married. You cannot wish to remain with a beast like him."

"She's mine," Arkain growls and Ryvik backs up even further.

"You see Ryvik, that's why a union between us would never work. You cling to our old traditions." I sidle up next to Arkain, gripping his hand and leaning into his side. "Would you still wish to marry me if I told you how many times King Arkain has fucked me between yesterday and today?"

Ryvik's face turns red. Trian looks me over with disgust, but I only press closer to Arkain, who tucks me into his side, baring his own fangs. "I didn't think so."

"You traitorous whore—"

Ryvik's tirade is cut short as an invisible force wraps around his throat. He claws at his neck, and Trian scrambles to try and help him but it is of no use.

"I am not a whore. I am the future queen of Myrkorvin. This beast" —I wrap my arms around Arkain—"gives me two things you never could. Protection and *pleasure*."

I kiss Arkain's cheek. "He's not worth the headache of killing." The magic choking Ryvik dissipates and he gasps for breath. Arkain's eyes are all predator.

"You have one hour to get across the bridge and into Lysan. If I find you lurking around here I'll kill you myself." With that final warning, Trian grabs Ryvik by his collar and the two disappear from the throne room.

My adrenaline leaves me as quickly as it came and my knees buckle. Arkain catches me, carrying me into a back room before setting me down in a chair. Handing me a glass of water, he strokes my hair as I drink.

"Elvie." Arkain's voice is soft. "You do not have to tell me if you do not wish to, but that male...did he ever hurt you?" I know what Arkain is implying and in truth, I understand his concerns. My reaction to seeing him. His concern loosens some of the tension in my chest.

"He never got the chance to," I say, drinking the last of my water. "Ryvik's favorite weapons were his words. He knew what to say at what time to inflict the most pain. My parents could see that and they dissolved the union shortly after it was announced." I set the glass down and smile up at him. "I liked seeing you all possessive over me. Made me all tingly."

Arkain laughs and helps me to my feet. "I'll show you possessive."

Leaning down, he captures my mouth, but before we can get too carried away there is another knock at the door.

"My king, the nobles are arriving."

"Nobles?" I ask.

Arkain sighs and pinches the bridge of his nose. "The messenger from last night brought word of the orcs' movements in the east. Any day now they could march on us. I have to inform the nobles and prepare their bannermen."

Cupping my cheek, he smiles down at me. "And officially announce you as my intended to all of them."

I return his smile softly. "Are you sure? That means you are never to take another. After our conversation this morning, you do not wish to wait for your mate?"

Arkain runs a clawed hand through my hair.

"I've lived a long time, Elvie. Long enough to know that this"—he gestures between us—"isn't normal. And whatever it is, I am grateful for it. I meant what I said before to Ryvik. You're mine. I want everyone to know it."

My smile is full of emotion as Arkain leans down towards me, pressing his gray lips against mine. The kiss is soft and heated and over far too soon for my liking.

CHAPTER TWENTY-THREE

ELVIE

DARK ELF NOBLES DIFFER FROM light elf nobles not only in appearance but in number.

The throne room is filled with dark and white hair alike. Gray skin and glowing red eyes. The female dark elves have rings on each finger, their claws filed down into long nails that are dyed red with some sort of lacquer. The men are dressed the same, their wealth on full display.

As I stand on the dais, I stand apart from them merely by the fact that I am not wearing black. Arkain stands next to me. Regal and proud. Wylan on his other side surveys the crowd with an appraising eye. Seeing everything and missing nothing.

One of the noble families steps forward and Arkain goes to greet them. The male is almost as tall as Arkain, with lines of age around his eyes, suggesting that he is easily approaching his tenth century. The female dark elf next to him is much younger. She must be his daughter. Her dark hair is cut sharply to her chin. She curtsies for Arkain, red eyes sparkling up at him under her thick black lashes.

I narrow my eyes at them as I feel Wylan press in on my side.

"That's Vysha," he says, nodding towards the female Arkain is speaking with. "She was the king's first love. He's always wanted to marry her and there was a rumor of a betrothal for years before his parents passed." I don't dignify him with a response.

"It seems as though the mutual affection is still there," he whispers and my eyes narrow in on them. Vysha leans against Arkain's side, whispering something in his ear that he shakes his head to. She gives him a

142

pout before winking and being whisked away by her father.

Before long, Arkain rejoins us on the dais and announces that dinner will be served in the dining hall. Threading my arm through his, we are the first to enter the hall. I cringe at all the roasted meats on display as Arkain and I make our way to the king's table near the front. Arkain sits at the center of the table that faces the rest of the room. I sit on his right and Wylan on his left.

A male lord takes a seat next to me and another fills on his other side. I watch as the dining room fills to bursting. While the nobles next to me begin to hack off chunks of greasy pork, a servant arrives with a steaming plate of vegetables for me and Arkain. My mouth waters and I squeeze his knee under the table.

"No meat for you, Your Grace?" The noble next to me asks Arkain.

"Princess Elveena does not eat meat, Lord Dashwyne. I did not want her to feel alone in it tonight."

"Doesn't eat meat?" Lord Dashwyne, as Arkain called him, nearly chokes on the mouthful he is chewing. He nudges the noble on his other side. "Grigor, did you hear that? The princess doesn't eat meat!"

"Really?" Grigor looks at me over Lord Dashwyne's shoulder. "No meat?"

"No meat," I say. "Very few light elves do."

"I knew you lot were a different breed," Grigor murmurs, and Arkain growls next to me before I kick him under the table. "Begging your pardon of course."

"It's nothing really, but if history is to be believed you all are the strange breed," I say while taking a sip of my wine.

"Tell us something, princess," one of the nobles from the gallery calls, "what were your first thoughts of Myrkorvin when you arrived here?"

The hall grows quiet as they wait for my response. Even Arkain looks at me as if to say *You are on your own with this one.*

"I thought it was very beautiful," I say. "I'd never left Lysan before and Myrkorvin, we are told, is wild and filled with creatures that will try and eat us."

"It is," someone shouts back and the hall laughs. I smile as well.

"But there is a beauty in the wildness of it. In truth, I do not know why my people fear you so much. The longer I stay here, the more I discover how alike our people are. Despite how different we may look."

"What is Lysan like these days? It has been centuries since we were able to travel there."

"It is warm—" I start to answer before another voice rings out.

"I do not remember female light elves being as beautiful as you."

Arkain tenses beside me and I give his knee another reassuring squeeze. That is how my dinner continues. Noble after noble peppers me with questions. About my time at the castle, growing up in Lysan, if I have any distant relatives that would be interested in taking a dark elf as a lover.

It is all in good fun but my voice is beginning to ache and as the meals are cleared away, the festivities of the dinner begin to die down. Arkain has been silent next to me for the better part of an hour. It does not take any thinking at all to surmise that he is jealous.

Turning towards him, I place my hand on his arm. "I want some attention." He sets his wine down and raises a brow at me.

"Seems like you were getting plenty of it from my nobles."

"But attention from you is the only attention I want," I say, leaning in to rub my nose along his cheek. I inhale his masculine scent and instantly my pussy gets wet. I can feel the eyes of the other nobles on us, and that's why it's important to make this show public. My beast needs to feel like he owns me, that his claim on me is known by everyone who sees us.

"Would you like me to show you how much I want attention from you?" I ask, dropping my hand to the hardening bulge in his pants. Arkain groans and stands, pulling me after him much to the dismay of Wylan and the curious looks of other nobles.

We are not the first to leave the dinner. Many lords and ladies are milling in the hall. Arkain pays them no mind as he pulls me into one of the alcoves, my purple ball gown swishing after me.

His claws snag in my hair as he ravages my mouth with his. Thrusting his tongue in, his rich taste fills my mouth. Growling against me, he pulls me hard to his chest, claws dig into my ass, and I moan into his mouth.

"You're mine," he says, licking down my neck. "They should not be allowed to even look at you. They covet what is mine, I know they do."

"But I am only yours. You're the only one I want," I pant as he grinds himself against me. There are voices coming closer and I freeze, but Arkain continues.

"Prove it and keep quiet," he says, before diving under my gown. My massive skirts keep him hidden as I feel his claws part my thighs and his tongue run along the seam of my pussy. Oh gods, he cannot be serious. I brace my hands on the wall of the alcove as Arkain's skillful tongue continues to work me.

"Princess Elveena," someone says behind me and I turn, almost tripping over the dark elf under my dress. It is Grigor from dinner.

"Hello," I say and my voice sounds breathless even to me.

"I just wanted to say that it was an honor to meet you this evening."

"Really?" I ask and swallow my moan as Arkain sucks on my clit.

"Yes, it has been so long since our two people shared a meal together. It would be nice if we could get back to the way things used to be, wouldn't you agree?"

"Oh yes," I breathe and Grigor's eyes widen. Surely he must smell what's going on beneath my skirts, but if he does he doesn't comment on it.

"Yes," I say again, trying to regain my composure. "That would be wonderful if our two peoples could reunite."

"Maybe you and the king could do that? You two seem fairly close." At that moment, Arkain decides to slip one of his fingers inside of me and my knees almost buckle.

"Yes," I grit out. "We are quite close."

"Speaking of the king, is he around here somewhere? There is a matter I must discuss with him…" He trails off and I seize this as my opportunity.

"King Arkain was headed towards the library last I saw him. Perhaps if you hurry you will catch him." Grigor thanks me and leaves. Now that we are alone Arkain doubles his efforts.

Alternating between plunging his tongue inside and two of his thick fingers, I lean my head against the nearest wall and moan. Pleasure courses through me and with one final nip at my clit I am done for. My thighs squeeze his head as I shake my way through a climax.

Crawling out from beneath my skirts, Arkain licks his lips with a self-satisfied smirk.

"Happy now?" I ask.

"Shouldn't I be asking you that?" I shake my head and link our arms together.

"Come, my beast. This party is only just getting started."

We make our way back into the great hall just as the band starts up. I look up at Arkain and he smiles, holding out his hand.

"Dance with me, princess?" His clawed hand envelopes mine and he leads me through each dance turn after turn, not stopping until the sun is painting the sky pink.

CHAPTER TWENTY-FOUR

ARKAIN

"YOUR MAJESTY, THEY ARE WAITING for your signal to begin the games." A page says from the other side of the tent.

I growl and that has him scurrying off. They can wait, I have more important matters to attend to. Like not spilling my seed down Elvie's throat as she works her mouth up and down my cock on her knees in front of me.

She is a gift. One I will cherish every single day. Her silver head bobs and spit dribbles down her chin as she takes me deeper into that warm, wonderful mouth of hers.

A mouth on my cock is not something I ever considered but now I do not know how I ever lived without it. I would let her suck me off all morning if we weren't already late. Besides, I need her coming on my cock if I am to make it through these games where I know males will be staring at her.

Perhaps they will covet her less when she has my seed spilling down her thighs.

I pull her from the floor, press her around and press her over a nearby table. Her cunt is pink and glistening and as I drag my cock through her folds, she moans into the wood, clawing at it with her blunt nails before I am slamming inside of her.

"We don't have much time, so be my good little elf and work your clit for me."

She moans as she does it, her small hand rubbing herself furiously as I pound into her. the lush curves of her ass cushion each slam of my hips. I dip the tip of my claw into her back entrance and she grows wetter.

"One day, I'll claim this hole too." And just like that, I feel her muscles begin to tighten, her cunt growing impossibly tighter as I continue to thrust into her. She cries out my name and I growl hers as my seed fills her. Pulling out, I watch it drip down her thighs and the beast inside me relaxes.

Tugging her gown back in place, her face is flushed and glowing as she smiles at me. I can take her to Lysan once a month and make her come as many times as she can stand and she will be happy. She will be mine.

Mine. Mine. *Mine.*

I would not be surprised if the word was written on my heart. Ever since our trip to Lysan, my possessiveness of her has grown. The depths of it I still do not know yet. If she is not with me, I seek her out. If she cannot go with me, it feels as though I am missing a part of myself until I have her in my arms again.

And my cock inside of her making her moan.

Exiting the tent, I keep her tucked close to my side. We pass a few nobles that are watching the games from my royal booth. Vysha and her father are two of them and they nod their respects as we pass.

Looking at her now it is hard to believe I considered what I felt for her at the time to be love. It is nowhere near close to what I feel for Elvie. I love Elvie. I know it to be true. I should tell her but this thing between us is so fresh. I know she desires me and wants me in her bed, but love?

I do not want to ruin my good fortune by saying something she isn't ready to hear. When the time is right I will tell her. For now I will enjoy her closeness and her smiles.

Leading Elvie to our seats I wave my hand and the games commence. Calling for an assembly of the nobles requires three parts as I explained to Elvie. A welcome dinner where we break bread and talk as friends, a contest of strength where the different lords and their banner-men show their prowess, and finally, court will be held where I will have to tell them what my scouts discovered in the east.

"Wylan told me about her," Elvie whispers next to me. She tips her head back towards Vysha and her father.

"Did he now?" I ask coldly, turning my attention down to the males sparing below. Elvie grabs my hand and squeezes it.

"He said you were betrothed once. That you loved her." Elvie reaches up and titls my chin down so I have to look at her. "I'd like to hear your version of events."

I sigh and realize I can deny her nothing.

"When I was younger and not what I am now, I believed myself to be in love with Vysha. At the time, she was the most beautiful elf I had ever seen. But she was as cruel as she was beautiful. On the night of my farewell party before I left to join the warriors to the east, I believed this to be my chance to make my feelings known. I told her that I wished her to be my betrothed and then when I returned I would wed her." I huff out a laugh. "She rejected me quite spectacularly. Sometimes I can still hear them laughing at me."

"Arkain, that's horrible." Elvie's grip on my hand tightens.

"It was. I know that now. And when I returned looking as I do now, she was the first one to approach me. To tell me she only scorned me to protect her image. That she had always cared for me. But I dismissed her in the same way she did me and even now she tries to get back in my good graces." I run a claw down Elvie's cheek. "Though now I think she's finally beginning to realize that she'll never be queen."

Elvie is quiet for a moment before saying, "Is she still the most beautiful elf you've ever seen?"

I laugh and tuck a strand of hair behind her pointed ear.

"No," I say, pressing a kiss to her brow. Glancing over her shoulder Elvie spies Vysha who is watching us through narrowed red eyes. Before I can guess her intent, Elvie leans over the arms of my throne and kisses me. Boldly. Making no mistake who owns me to anyone who's watching. It's easy to be sucked into these moments with her, but the reality of what's to come makes me break the kiss.

"Tonight I will tell the nobles they are to prepare for war. Another scout arrived this morning and the orcs march towards us." Elvie's eyes grow concerned. "And I want to marry you before I leave for war. To make it abundantly clear to everyone while I am gone who you belong to." I pause. "I know the chances of you being with child are slim, but my heir could be growing inside you now. I will have both you and our child shielded by the bonds of our marriage."

"Arkain." Her silver eyes are wet and I shake my head.

149

"Let us enjoy today and I will make preparations for tonight."

Elvie nods and snuggles into my side. If I could, I would stay here with her like this forever. But the orcs move toward us and I will do whatever I must to make sure she is safe.

CHAPTER TWENTY-FIVE

ELVIE

ARKAIN LEFT OUR BED EARLY this morning to go out hunting with the nobles.

So instead of waiting around for him like a loyal dog, I find myself in Kaethe's lab, helping her with last-minute ingredients to assist with her orc's teeth poison antidote. We are quiet as we work. Kae is sifting more liverworms through a fine mesh sieve and I am trying to grow more to replace our dwindling supply.

Kae sighs and holds up the glass container.

"I only have a small bit of the poison to test against. So my chances of getting this right are slim." Her face hardens. "And if the orcs do march toward us then I hope King Arkain sends them all back to whatever hell they escaped from."

That stops me. Kae is normally curious, if a little snappy. Never have I heard her speak with such anger before.

"Did something happen between you and an orc?" I ask. Kaethe's hands freeze on the glass tube and I am afraid she's going to shatter it.

"It's just that all of this seems quite personal, so I just assumed…" I trail off. "Don't mind me, I haven't been getting much sleep.

"I know. The whole castle can hear you two," She sighs. "When I was a girl, my family and I lived in a village outside of Moonbourne. Life was typical, easy. Until one night my father heard a noise outside and didn't come back in. My mother hid me and my brother in the cellar but it didn't keep out her screams."

Kae shakes herself as if from a particularly bad memory.

"Orcs raided our village, my brother and I escaped, but in our panic I lost him in the woods. I do not know if he is still alive or what became of him. I hope he is still alive but I just don't know…" She trails off and I grip her shoulder.

"You were very brave, Kaethe. You still are." We sit in silence for a moment before I add, "Is the antidote ready to test yet?"

Kae shakes her head. "This new experiment requires me to let the mixture ferment for twenty-four hours. Once it is done, by the gods I hope it works."

"If anyone is going to figure it out it's you, Kae."

"Gods I hope you are right. Let's just hope the orcs haven't developed any new weapons since the last time they fought a war."

Pushing through the doors to our room, the last thing I expect to find is Arkain.

Sweaty and shirtless and back from his hunt, I almost think I am in for an afternoon tumble in the sheets. His grave face stops me. Icy fear trickles down my back.

"Our scouts sent word, the Orcs are almost at Moonbourne. Our nobles have already sent the bannermen here with them east to fortify our lands. The rest of their houses will ride out to join them. The orcs will be there in two days' time and it takes almost that long to get to Moonbourne."

"When will you leave?" I ask, my voice barely above a whisper.

"At first light."

"But what about us?" My chest is beginning to ache. "I just found you, I can't lose you."

"Elvie," Arkain says, coming to stand at my side. "The gods themselves could not pull me away from you. But I am king and I have to ride out with my men."

He is leaving in the morning. My king, my beast, my Arkain. My love. Riding out to face an enemy that decimated his forces last time. The gods could not have brought us together only for war to tear us apart.

Perhaps they are not convinced of our union being true. We must honor it to them before he leaves. Lest they deem him not worthy of protecting.

"We will marry," I say but he shakes his head.

"I contacted the priest. The fastest he could get here would be tomorrow evening. I am sorry, Elvie. If there was another way—"

"There is another way. You are a king are you not?"

"Yes?"

"Then you can marry us. In the way of the First Gods. How our kind married before there were priests."

"Elvie, a marriage made directly in the name of the gods is not something that can ever be broken. Are you sure that is what you wish?"

"I am yours and you are mine. I will have it be known to all the gods that our pairing is true." I start to unlace my dress while Arkain remains rooted in his spot. "You do know how to perform the ritual, don't you?"

"Yes," he whispers as he begins to disrobe as well. Soon we are naked in front of the roaring fire. Knees pressed together, digging into the soft carpet. The small knife Arkain bestowed to me is in my hand. I drag the blade across my palm and watch the blood swell.

"I offer you my blood," I say and watch as my blood sizzles on the burning logs. Arkain does the same as me. Picking up a piece of one of my favorite gowns, I watch it blacken in the flames and turn to dust.

"I offer you my possessions." Arkain throws a scrap of leather from his armor and repeats the phrase after me.

"Dear gods," Arkain says, "as your appointed monarch and wielder of the free magic, I come to you today to take this female as my bride. To have her and keep her. To take no other beside her. To lay my life down for her. To make her mine from this day until my final day."

The flames crackle as if hearing his proclamation. I repeat the passage back and the flames crackle for me as well.

"Take from us these offerings that our union is true," I say, tossing a bouquet of wildflowers into the flame. The symbol of our first meeting. Arkain and I gaze at each other as the flames warm us. There is a finality in the words that are spoken here.

For all that led us to this point, I have no regrets. I love him. And I will be damned if the gods take him from me before we've even gotten a chance to start our lives together.

"Now we honor our vow to you with our bodies." Arkain's red eyes glow in the firelight as he leans down to kiss me. There is a tenderness to his touch and I refuse to believe it is his way of saying goodbye. His kiss his devastatingly soft, his tongue languid as it dances with mine.

Our movements are slow and unhurried. He gently pries my legs apart, running a claw along my slit to deem me wet enough to take him. There, on the carpet in front of the hearth, Arkain claims me in the old way. With the gods as our witnesses and our bodies their vessels to bestow the blessings.

He moves inside me over and over again. Each thrust is as devastating as the last and I do not realize I am weeping until Arkain wipes the moisture from my eyes. I cling to him in this moment. As if he is the only thing tethering me to this plane.

My muscles tense as do Arkain's, and with one last mighty thrust, my muscles clamp down around him as he gives me his final offering to the gods. Our union is complete.

A satisfied grin spreads over my face as we lie in the afterglow.

"How was that, wife? Didn't know I could be so gentle, did you?" The endearment tickles me and I turn to snuggle into his side.

"I prefer your rougher side, husband. But it's nice to know you can do both."

We laugh quietly and resume our comfortable silence. Until a squawk at the window makes us both shoot up.

There perched on the ledge is a golden seagull. The official messenger bird of Lysan. Rising, I pad over to the creature and gently unclip the tiny scroll he has tied to his foot.

My stomach drops as I read my mother's elegant script.

"Elvie what is it?" Arkain asks, coming to stand beside.

"It's my father," my voice is shaky. "He has fallen ill, our healers say he may not make it to see in the morning."

Dropping the note, I rush to the wardrobe, ripping clothes off the shelves. I slip my legs into a pair of riding pants and rummage around to find a pair of sturdy boots. I pick up the knife from in front of the fire and tuck it into my boot.

"What are you doing?" Arkain asks.

"I have to leave for Lysan at once. If I use the portal, I can be there before sundown."

"No." My mind is cycling through a million different thoughts that I barely hear what Arkain says. But when I register what he just said I paused in my tracks.

"No what?"

"No, you will not travel to Lysan. I forbid it," he says and I turn and face his molten red eyes.

CHAPTER TWENTY-SIX

ARKAIN

S HE WANTS TO LEAVE. I ride out to meet my greatest enemy and she wants to leave.

I know my fears are irrational. I know after all that we have been through I shouldn't be holding on to these old insecurities but I cannot help it. If I allow her to go, she will never return. I feel it in my bones.

There is something not right here. Something about this feels wrong. Not just her wanting to leave but this whole situation has my beast rattling around in my chest. If she goes she will not come back. For all that I trust her, I do not trust this situation.

Something is trying to take her from me, I know it.

She is mine. The beast inside me growls in agreement, it does not want her to leave either. Now she is staring at me, seething with her small fangs bared at me.

"What do you mean, you are forbidding me from going home?"

"Exactly what I said," I say. I have to keep firm even though it cuts me to see her look at me with such disdain in her eyes. "You are to remain in Myrkorvin. That is my order to you."

"You do not give me orders!" she shouts.

"Yes, I do! As your king and as your husband, I command you to stay inside this castle until I return."

She scoffs at me and shakes her head. "If that is how you view the vows we just made then you are no better than Ryvik." She goes to grab one of the satchel bags I have hanging but I grasp her wrist. "Let me go."

I drop my hand but press on. "How do you know this isn't some trick? Your father was in fine health three weeks ago and now he has some mysterious illness that will take him before the moon rises?" She glares at me but continues stuffing things into the bag.

"I wouldn't question it if it were you." That thought warms me but I cannot let her leave. I just got her, I cannot lose her already.

"What are you so afraid of? I can tell that's what this is. You only get this irrational and pig-headed when you are scared. So what is it, Arkain?" She stands there with her hand on her hips. Gods, she is so beautiful. And fierce and loyal.

It's obvious I never deserved her.

"How can I be sure that the moment you get home you never wish to return? That you realize that there is nothing for you here to return to."

"I have you to return to."

"And you expect me to believe that's a good enough reason for you to come back?"

"You do not believe my feelings for you are true?" Her words are wounded. My emotions are high and I am panicking. Of course I know she is genuine. Isn't she?

"Maybe you saw me for the lonely king I was and decided that I was a safe bet. A king you could placate with sweet words and soft touches and I would give you the power you were so hungry for."

Her slap sounds worse than it feels. But it does the trick in breaking me from my insecure ramblings. I open my mouth to take it back. To tell her that she can...go?

But no, I cannot allow it. No matter how much I hate how she's looking at me. Something about this is off.

"If that is how you truly see me," she says in a cold voice I have never heard before. "then perhaps it is best if I never return."

She turns on a heel and flees the room, and I let her. Even with my beast pushing me to grab her, keep her. Until I can get to the root of all of this, I am powerless to do anything but what I've always done when it comes to Elvie.

Give her exactly what she wants.

CHAPTER TWENTY-SEVEN

ELVIE

My MIDNIGHT STALLION FLIES FROM the castle towards Last-light forest.

The brutal wind rips at my hair and stings my face. But my tears are not from the wind. They are from Arkain and his inability to think himself worthy of love.

I know he didn't mean what he said to me, but it hurt all the same. He is so scared that I am going to leave him, that he'd rather push me away. And let's face it, he did a pretty fantastic job of it.

My horse trots to the clearing and a fresh wave of tears threaten to spill. The last time I was here I was so happy. Now I am at odds with my husband and my father is dying.

My father. I cannot let this fight with Arkain overshadow my purpose for being out here. Mother's note was brief but her pleading was clear. To get there as soon as possible. I gallop through the forest, my steed avoiding the large branches of the trees.

I try not to think of the predators that lurk here as the portal comes into sight. Without giving myself a chance to reconsider, I urge my horse forward and we dive through it at full speed.

Emerging in Merrywood forest, I remember Arkain's pleading to keep this portal a secret. I'll tell my family I was already on my way home for a visit when a rider came upon me with their message. Though if my father's condition is as bad as they've stated, I doubt they'll be asking me how I got here so fast.

As my horse gallops faster, I find it odd that the first time I am back in Lysan alone, all I wish is to be back in Myrkorvin. In bed with Arkain, exploring each other and telling stories. Even now that my heart is breaking for my father, it still yearns for my husband.

One that rides off to war at first light.

My stomach plummets. He will be alright. He has to be. When I return to Myrkorvin we will work this out and come to a better understanding. That he is worthy of my love and he shouldn't think that it is some trick.

I am so deep in thought that I do not even realize I am at Solys until my horse's hooves clap on the stone path. Dismounting and tethering him to a post by the door, I push the door open and yell out.

"Mother? Father? Briar?" I call. "Garren?"

My boot clad feet squeak on the tile. The palace is eerily quiet. It is odd that no other lords from neighboring territories are here to pay their respects. Something doesn't feel right here, the hairs on the back of my neck are raising. Still, I push into the throne room.

Only to be greeted by the sight of both my parents.

At first I am elated that my father looks so well, until unease curls my stomach. I notice their hands tied to their thrones. The fabric around their mouths. My two brothers are bound and gagged in the corner. Sybil is nowhere to be found. I hope that means she was not here when whatever this is went down.

"What is going on?" I ask, but my parents just shake their heads.

"I believe I can answer that." That oily voice makes my skin crawl. I turn and see Ryvik leaning against one of the walls. Still dressed in the clothes I saw him in a few days ago. Trian stands to his left baring his teeth at me.

"You see Elvie, this is quite simply all your fault. If you hadn't been such a little slut and married me like you were supposed to, all of this could've been avoided." He laughs. "I would've bedded, bred you, and at least had the decency to make killing your family look like an accident before assuming the throne."

He walks over to my parents and pinches my father's cheek, who bares his teeth as much as he can. Ryvik only chuckles and descends back towards me.

"But then dear old dad just had to send you off to Myrkorvin. And you opened your legs to that beast and he ruined everything, and now I have to kill him. And his kingdom will be mine by right."

"You're insane," I spit. "What makes you think you're even capable of killing Arkain?"

Ryvik's smile is all teeth and he gestures towards Trian who digs around in his satchel.

"It was a hard artifact to find and it costs a lot of fucking gold marks but it was worth it." Trian pulls the object out of his bag and my heart sinks before Ryvik even says what it is. "An orc's teeth arrow. Terribly hard to come by, but extremely poisonous."

I try my best to be brave, even while my heart pounds in my chest. I have to keep him talking. Ryvik loves to hear himself talk, and maybe I can get him to reveal a part of his plan that will help me free my parents and save Arkain.

"So what is your plan? To sneak into Myrkorvin and assassinate the king? How will that win you his kingdom?"

"Our bannermen have already rallied to enter Myrkorvin. Did you know Trian can copy anyone's handwriting almost perfectly? He replicated your mother's to get you here, and a few hundred scrolls to Lysan nobles posing as your father. Beseeching them to ride north to save his precious daughter who was being defiled nightly by that beast of a king. The same king who tried to murder me, one of Lysan's golden sons, in cold blood for trying to save you."

"Our forces are nowhere near the size of Myrkorvin's, they'll be slaughtered immediately."

"Perhaps if Arkain hadn't already sent his bannermen east that would be true." I snap up my head and look at Ryvik. His grin only deepens. "They'll be off fighting the orcs. Or at least thinking they are. By the time any of them figure out it was a trick, King Arkain will be dead."

"Why the *fuck* are you doing this?" I scream. Ryvik lets out a shrill whistle and two strong guards come in and grasp me around the upper arms. "I'll find a way to warn Arkain!"

"I severely doubt that. Keep her in her room. The free magic will be out of her system soon." His teeth flash as he smiles at me. "That's when the real fun will begin."

I've been pacing this room for hours, trying to think of any way I can escape.

My windows and doors have been warded shut. My power was useless against them initially. Now with the free magic completely out of my system it is no use to keep trying. My head is whirling with so many questions.

Mainly, how did Ryvik get embroiled in something like this? Sure he's always been a snake but treason? He never seemed ambitious enough for that. Now, he's armed with an orc's teeth arrow and is determined to murder my husband. I have to get out of here and tell Arkain about Ryvik's plan.

Most importantly, the threat of the orcs isn't real.

My door swings open and in walks Ryvik. I stand in the corner of the room and he chuckles, not even bothering to close the door. That's how little of a threat he views me as. The little knife in my boot Arkain gave me feels like the only way I am going to make him regret that.

"Gods, you even smell like that foul creature," Ryvik huffs. "Either he must be breeding you regularly or he's your mate. The gods can be cruel."

I glare at him and spit, "Arkain is double the male you are."

"He's also about to be twice as dead as I am."

"Even if the bannermen leave now, it takes a few hours to get to Blackfire Castle." I gesture towards the rising sun. "Arkain is leaving at first light to go east. You'll miss your chance to kill him." I hope.

"See that is where you are wrong, Elvie. As we speak, our bannermen are pouring through the portal deep in the Merrywood. They'll surround Myrkorvin and wait for my signal before they launch their attack." My heart splinters and my shoulders slump. "Oh? Did you think I didn't know about the portal? How do you think Arkain will react when he finds out we've used it and you're the only light elf that knew about it?"

Ryvik tsks. "Even if you did somehow manage to get word to him about my plan, why would he believe the words of a traitor?"

Something snaps inside of me and I snarl, launching myself at him with my claws. Ryvik catches me and slams me down on the bed as I try my best to kick him with my boots.

"Before I leave, I might as well sample the King's bride. I'll tell him all about it when I cut him down with that poison—"

One of my kicks lands and it sends Ryvik back a few steps. Before he gets a chance to think, I grab for the knife in my boot. Pressing down on the button and watching the blade slide out, I strike and my knife embeds itself in Ryvik's chest.

His golden eyes are wide. His mouth is open as if to say something, but no words come out as blood trickles from the corner of his mouth. I gasp and let his body fall to the ground.

I killed an elf. I killed an elf. I killed an elf.

If I am to become a dark elf, then at least I have Arkain. Who I need to warn, and I pray to the gods that he believes me. Ryvik said that the bannerman were waiting for his signal to invade. I look down at his corpse and swallow the bile that rises in my throat back down.

I know what I have to do, and if I've already damned myself…I just hope that I'm not too late.

CHAPTER TWENTY-EIGHT

ARKAIN

THE NIGHT SKY FADES FROM its inky black to a pale pink.

Dawn is here and I am still a fool. Gods, how could I have been so stupid to say those things to her? I should've offered to go to Lysan with her. Her family is my family now.

But instead, I called into question her feelings for me. Her character. When I should've been telling her how much I loved her. That even if this was all the time we had together it was more than I ever deserved.

Now it seems like I've ruined any chance of getting to right this wrong.

There is a sharp bang at my door. For a moment, I think it is Elvie but the voice on the other side quickly dashes those hopes.

"Your Majesty, this is urgent," Aiko's voice sounds grave. Oh gods, what now?

"What is it? A new development in the east?" I ask. "Is it Elvie?"

"It's—I can't believe I'm saying this, there are—"

"Light elves pouring out of Lastlight forest. Armed to the teeth and ready for battle. I'll give you one guess as to who tipped them off to the portal in the forest."

My knees grow weak and my vision darkens. Light elves pouring out of Lastlight. Elvie. She…betrayed me?

"It would appear that way, Your Majesty." I had not realized I had spoken that sentence out loud.

"I told you she was not to be trusted, now we have invaders at our door calling for your head." Wylan rakes a claw down his face. "Thank the gods you did not marry her or this kingdom would fall to her as queen."

My silence makes Wylan curse. "Fucking fool."

My Elvie. The one who smiled with me and danced with me by the glowing willow. Who read with me every night in the library, and let me kiss her in my dining room. Who told me she was mine and that I was hers.

She has betrayed me. Just like my father always said. To let something go, is to lose it forever. I have lost Elvie. Did I ever really have her?

I can't dwell on that now, even has my heart threatens to shatter in my chest. My kingdom needs its warrior king, not a male who's been played for fool. A calmness settles over me as I look at Aiko and Wylan.

"How many males do they have?"

"A few hundred," Aiko responds.

"And how many do we have?"

"Including the new recruits, I'd say maybe one hundred."

I nod and move to my armor chest. "Find anyone who can fight and bring them to the west side of the castle. We are not going down without a fight."

With ice in my veins and a broken heart, I prepare myself to defend my castle once more.

CHAPTER TWENTY-NINE

ELVIE

MY HORSE HAS TO BE exhausted, but gods bless him he keeps galloping.

We cross through the portal and his hooves are the only thing keeping me grounded. I have to make it in time. If I can get there before they start fighting and before I start turning into a dark elf, everyone may be able to walk away without spilling any blood.

The weight in my satchel makes my stomach churn but it had to be done.

My horse continues his sprint and I can see the edge of the forest. Breaking through into the clearing, the sight freezes my blood. A sea of golden armor stares down a measly gathering of black. Arkain is easy enough to spot atop his proud horse. By the way some of the figures in black tremble holding the sword in their hand, they have to be new recruits.

Arkain's face is cold and distant. Seeing him in this way convinces me that I was too late in stopping Ryvik's lies from reaching him. I pray to the gods that there is still time for me to convince him of my innocence.

I hear Trian's voice on the wind. "These monsters defiled your princess. Their king kept her and brutalized her. Just as they have kept us away from our ancestral lands for centuries. It is in her name today that we lead the charge." A chorus of cheers go up and I know I have to act now.

Kneeing my steed in the sides he takes off again and I blaze a trail down the center of the clearing between the two sides. Arkain's eyes track me as I get closer but they are like cold fire. The warmth in them has been put out. Wylan's face does not even try to conceal his contempt.

165

"As the princess whose name you are fighting for today I urge you, my people, to put down your weapons," I call out. "You have been lied to. King Arkain never hurt me. He treated me with kindness. With compassion."

"She lies!" Trian yells. "Look at how his seed has polluted her. To try and make us feel sorry for these beasts. She probably carries his spawn within her now."

I stare back at my people, Trian's words ringing in my ears as I rest a hand on my stomach.

"If I do, I would welcome mine and the king's child. He would be a wonderful father." I turn to look at Arkain but he will not even look at me. The pain in my chest yawns open and I realize I have to go through with my plan.

"My people, Ryvik tricked you. My father never sent you those letters that I was being harmed. Trian forged them. Sent you all here so that Ryvik could kill King Arkain and claim the throne. This was never about honoring my family."

"More lies," Trian yells.

"It is the truth. And I'll prove it to you." Reaching inside the satchel, my fingers catch on soft blonde hair. Lifting it high above my head for all to see, the crowd gasps at Ryvik's severed head that dangles from my hand. "I killed him for his treachery. Paying the ultimate sacrifice of taking a life to prove that he was lying."

I look around the crowd. "Go home to your families. Hold them tight. There is no need for any more blood to be spilled today."

The silence stretches on, then slowly, one by one the golden warriors turn and make their way back through the forest. I let out a breath and laugh. It worked. Thank the gods it worked. Turning back toward the castle, I trot over to Arkain.

Once I am in front of him, he yanks off his helmet and those red eyes chill me to my bone. He says nothing, but Wylan is ready to strike.

"Do not think that we will be swayed by this little performance." I ignore him and try to meet Arkain's eyes.

"I never betrayed you."

"Then how did they know about the portal?" His tone is clipped.

"Ryvik said someone else told him and he told the others."

"You honestly expect us to believe that?" Wylan scoffs.

"It's the truth, please, Arkain," I plead but his eyes remain cold and distant. With every passing moment I feel as though I have lost him to a place I'll never get him back from. The silence stretches until he finally speaks.

"Our marriage was done in front of the gods and cannot be undone. You have fulfilled your end of the bargain from the Night of a Hundred Faces. Nothing is tethering you here anymore. You are free to go wherever you please."

"Yes, there is something tying me here—" But Arkain turns from me, intent on walking back to the castle and away from me forever. I go to call for him again when a scream pierces the air.

Trian is galloping towards us. My stomach plummets when I see the orc's teeth arrow notched in his bow. And aimed directly at Arkain's heart. There's no time to warn him, no time shout. Instinct moves me as I leap from my horse into the path of the careening arrow.

The arrow embeds itself into my shoulder and the pain is instant. Like a hot iron is being pushed through my bone. Kaethe was right, this does make me want to beg for death. My vision is blurring but I can just make out Arkain approaching Trian…before grabbing him by the shoulders and ripping him in half, blood and gore hitting the ground with soft thuds.

Even with the pain, I still manage to shudder. *At least I got to see that before I died.*

Then he is at my side. Cradling me in his arms. One final time it would seem. From all of Kaethe's research, I know I don't have long to go now.

"Why?" It's all he can seem to say. "Why? Why? Why?"

I smile and groan at the pain. My vision is growing dark but I manage to say it anyway.

"You know why." A broken sob leaves him and my vision goes dark but at least I think I am able to get out the words.

"I love you."

CHAPTER THIRTY

ELVIE

I EXPECTED DEATH TO BE A lot more peaceful than this.

Every few seconds I am roused from a deep sleep to the feeling of someone prodding and poking me. Every once in a while I can just make out Kaethe muttering about how it will work this time. I wish she would just let me sleep. Her earthy scent tickles my nose.

Other times it is Arkain's voice. Deep and rough as if he has been screaming. He pleads with me to open my eyes. That he cannot lose me. That he's sorry. So *fucking* sorry.

That's the one that I finally try to crawl towards, but I feel as though my body is moving in honey. I have to keep going, but resting sounds so nice…

My eyes fly open and I do not know where I am. Looking left I see Arkain, squeezed into a tiny chair that looks incredibly uncomfortable. He holds my hand and I give it a gentle squeeze. Now his eyes fly open.

"Elvie," he breathes. I try to speak but the air rasps out of me. "Shhhh, don't try and talk just yet." He hands me a glass of water that I down in one go. He refills it for me and I down that one as well. Gods, why am I so thirsty?

After my fifth glass, I wave off another refill.

"You've been out for two days. I'm not surprised you are so dehydrated."

Two days? The pain in my shoulder comes on suddenly but that's not the only thing I remember.

"My—" I break off, coughing. "Parents. Trapped."

"Shhhh Elvie, I sent guards to your house and they freed your parents. They're here resting." He strokes his claw over my cheek and tangles it in my hair. My shoulder pain starts throbbing and I wince. "It should hurt for the next couple days but you should make a full recovery."

"Kae's antidote worked?" I whisper, relieved to have my voice back.

"Not quite." Arkain turns grim. "What that light elf had was a very good knock-off, but not the same strain as true orc's teeth poison. Had it been the real thing…"

He cups my cheek and presses a kiss to my forehead.

"Arkain you have to listen to me," I say and he nods. I walk him through everything from Ryvik's plan to assassinate him, to them rallying the Lysan's bannermen, to there not really being any rumblings of an orc uprising.

"You have to believe I'd never betray you, Arkain. Never."

"I know you wouldn't and I am so sorry for believing even for a moment that you would. Knowing that I hurt you makes me sick. Elvie, when you jumped in front of that arrow for me…I've never felt fear like that." He shakes his head. "I still don't understand why you would've done that."

"Yes you do." I run my finger along the curve of his ear but he shakes his head again. It's the only logical explanation. Why I feel for him so strongly the way that I do. Why my body moved on its own accord to save him. "You don't believe I am your mate?"

"I don't believe I am that lucky."

I laugh and swat his arm. "Well, believe it."

"I love you. I've known for so long but was afraid to tell you. From now on I'm telling you every day." He bends down to press a gentle kiss to my lips. "I love you, Elvie. Queen of Myrkorvin. My wife. My mate."

"I love you too," I say, and pat the cot next to me. "Now get up here and show me how sorry you are for doubting."

"I don't want to hurt you."

"You say that every time."

"This time is different. We shouldn't be putting pressure on your shoulder…" He trails off as I slip the white cotton gown over my head leaving myself bare to his eyes. He growls and gently grasps one of my breasts. He bends down to lick my nipple until it's a hard peak. Then he gives the other one the same treatment. His head pops up. "If anything hurts we stop immediately, yes?"

"Sure," I say, guiding his face back down my body. He pulls me to his chest and then rotates us so he is on his back and I am sitting atop his hardening cock.

"I can feel you soaking through my pants. Two days without my cock and this is what you turn into?"

I whine and rub myself against the bulge in his pants. "I want it. Please."

"You always beg so nicely when you want my cock, mate."

He unlaces himself and the sight of him makes my thighs clench. The pain in my shoulder is forgotten and now all I want is to feel him stretch me.

Raising me gently, he lowers me back down on his cock inch by glorious inch. My toes curl and I throw my head back. He leans forward to capture my nipple in his mouth as he continues to raise and lower me on his length, all the while punching his hips up to meet mine.

It is slow and it is brutal. It's exactly what I need. I dig my nails into his chest and take over at my own place, raising and slamming myself back down. Circling and grinding him so that my clit rubs against him.

The pleasure gathers in my stomach and my muscles tense.

"I'm close," I moan and Arkain rears up to capture my mouth.

"Every day for the rest of eternity I am going to fill you with my seed. Over and over again. Even once I get you pregnant I'm going to fill you. So there's no doubt in your mind or anyone else's who this tight cunt belongs to." He bends down and embeds his teeth in my neck. He groans around my flesh. "My mate, my beautiful mate."

I choke on my moan as he fucks me over and again, slamming me down on his cock. My body jolting and my breasts bouncing. The pleasure is too much, too intense.

"Arkain, I can't hold it I'm going to—"

"Tell me what I want to hear and I'll let you come." My eyes fly open and I look deep into his, wrapping my arms around his shoulders as he continues to pound into me.

"I love you," I say and he roars, a claw snaking down to tickle my clit and I'm up in flames. White-hot fire coats my body and the pleasure seems never-ending.

I lie boneless in a heap on the cot. Warm and safe and protected in Arkain's arms. But something tickles in my mind and before sleep claims me, I have to ask, "How long does it take to transform into a dark elf?"

Arkain tucks my head under his chin, "What?"

"It's just that I thought it was instantaneous after you killed another elf that you became one, but it seems my transformation is taking its time."

"Who told you killing an elf was how you become a dark elf?"

"It's what we are taught…" I can feel his body shaking with laughter under me. "Is that not right?"

"No, that's not right. The killing has to be unjust. Under the blood moon. That happens only once every two hundred years."

"Oh, well, someone should really update our tutors with that information." I snuggle deeper into Arkain's warm chest.

"I do have to say the thought of you biting me with dark elf fangs does make my cock hard."

"Really?"

"Yes."

"I can bite you now."

"Go to sleep, my little mate."

CHAPTER THIRTY-ONE

ARKAIN

THERE ARE FAR TOO MANY people who are close to my mate.

Even if they are her family, and by extension my family, they are still too close for my liking. Especially how they move and fuss around her. That is my job, one I will cherish to the end of my days.

After waking up on top of me in the cot, Elvie proclaimed herself fine enough for a real bed and demanded she be transferred to one immediately. So now here we all are in Elvie's old chambers, as Kaethe finishes up her examination on her shoulder.

The wound should heal completely but the scar will be prominent.

"That's fine," Elvie had said before wiggling her eyebrows at me, "as long as you promise to kiss it every night." I told her I would kiss her scar and a whole lot more to which her brother Garren turned a muted shade of green.

The whole Lysan royal family is in here. Even Wylan popped in to thank her for saving my life and the kingdom. I've seen people more grateful for *beaverviper* bites than he seemed, but Elvie did not seem too worried about it.

He has just left when King Orvian and Queen Mirella ask if they can have an audience with just me and Elvie. Garren looks like he's ready to argue but one glance at Elvie's shoulder and he stands, guiding his mate out of the room, with Briar following closely behind and shutting the door.

"What is it?" Elvie asks. Her parents eye each other warily before her mother goes to the bag she has stowed in the corner since she first entered. She pulls out what looks to be an envelope with the seal broken.

172

"Once King Arkain's men freed us, we went to survey the damage done to the house. In Elvie's room is where we found...what was left of Ryvik." King Orvian pauses and then nods and the queen hands me the envelope. "It states that they will have three days before the bannermen report back saying that the claims of orc uprisings were false. That you, Arkain need to be dead by then."

My blood runs cold as I look at the note, I'd recognize that script anywhere.

"Wylan."

How could I have been so blind? There is only one person who coordinates the scouts. Who has them report directly to him before the message is relayed to me. All this time he pretended to be my closest advisor only to be waiting to stab me in the back.

"Have you shown these to anyone else?" I ask, and King Orvian shakes his head.

"Let's keep this between us for now."

"What are you going to do?" Elvie asks. I look down at her and kiss her forehead.

"Something that makes him see me for the beast I truly am."

The throne room is filled with nobles and their bannermen.

I sit on my metal throne with Elvie draped in my lap, her bandaged shoulder peeking out from the sleeve of her dress. She looks as beautiful as ever.

Her parents and siblings are off to the side looking nervous. Wylan is positioned next to them, his back ramrod straight and proud. Right, it's time. I help Elvie stand as I make my way to the front of the dais. The crowd grows quiet as I look at them all.

"It was a close call two nights ago, but as a show of good faith between Light and dark elves, King Orvian is here to solidify the union between his daughter and me. This union will bring along the peaceful alliance of our two people. To usher us into a new age." I harden my voice. "But this new age cannot be attained until we snuff out the mole in our ranks."

The crowd turns to each other and murmurs. Wylan doesn't budge but I can notice the sweat beading at his brow.

"Send him in," I call and the oak doors open reveal my much awaited guest.

"Please reveal yourself to us."

"I am a knight for the House of Nightspears, Your Majesty."

"House Nightspears is one of our own most eastern reaches, correct?"

"Yes, my king."

"And tell us what sort of disturbances you have heard in the orc tunnels?"

"Nothing, my king. All is quiet, the orcs do not stir."

"Not stirring at all. You see my people? These whispers of orc uprisings were lies. Perpetrated by someone who wanted us weakened for the light elf invasion. Someone who has always been close to the crown." I turn my red stare at Wylan who rears back. "Seize him."

"What is the meaning of this? Unhand me!" Wylan splutters as my guards take hold of him. "Arkain what is the meaning of this? You are mistaken if you think I've plotted against you!"

"Are you calling your king a liar?" I ask.

"That light elf bitch has corrupted you."

"You mean my wife and my mate who took an orc's teeth arrow in the shoulder to save my life, while you plotted to end it? That light elf bitch?" I jump down from the dais and loom over him. "What did I say would happen if you ever spoke about her in that way again?" With a wave of my hand, the metallic taste of magic coats my tongue and Wylan howls as both his ankles and wrists are snapped.

"You should've never thrown that ball!"

"Oh?"

"I had been consolidating power for years. While you were out playing soldier I was running things. Then you had the bright idea to throw that ball and suddenly I'm back to square one. Forced to ally with a dimwitted light elf to finally claim my kingdom."

"Why, Wylan?" I ask. "After all these years, why betray me now?"

"Because you were never meant to be king! Your father promised it to me if he could not sire an heir. But then you were born and I knew I had no chance to rule unless I took matters into my own hands. You should've stayed weak, those poisons I was giving you should've killed you!"

There is a shocked cry amongst those in the crowd but I smile at Wylan like a wolf who finally caught the rabbit.

"Drop him at the orc tunnels. Tell them it's a peace offering."

Wylan continues to wail as he is dragged from the throne room. Elvie comes to stand beside me and I wrap her in my arms. Together, we will forge that new path and I will kill anyone that threatens that.

CHAPTER THIRTY-TWO

ELVIE

IT IS MY CORONATION DAY and Blackfire Castle is putting even Solys to shame.

My family is here along with most of our lords and ladies. Arkain has kept his word and today signifies the beginning of a new union between our people. The road to forgiveness is long, but can only begin by taking the first step.

As I wait outside to be called forward, I look down at my gold gown and smile. My mother had it specially made for today. Sitting at my vanity in the queen's room, my mother expertly twisted and curled my hair, just as she had before the night the ball that changed everything.

"You look beautiful, my dear. A true—"

"Queen this time." Her soft laughter tickles my ears. "Look at us. Two queens."

"But still mother and daughter," she said. "And as a good mother I am required to ask, you are still being safe, aren't you?"

"Mother!"

"I know you are married now but from the way you two stare at each other—"

"MOTHER!"

"Your father and I were the same way, believe me, sometimes I could scarcely bathe before the male was—"

"I am not having this conversation with you. I am being safe. I love him very much. That is all."

"And you are happy?"

I smile softly. "The happiest I have ever been."

The truth of that statement warms me. Life seemed so cut and dry for me before but with Arkain, everyday is an adventure. A chance to learn about something new. Visit someplace new. That's my first royal act as queen, to open the bridge to all.

The orchestra swells and I know it is time. The oak doors pull open and reveal quite the sight. The throne room is packed, dark and light elves mixed together. Both of our kinds turning to face me as I walk down the red carpet towards the dias. The throne room is decorated in red and gold candles, as well as dozens of wildflower arrangements from the royal garden. It's perfect.

I continue forward, my gold dress and red cape that matches Arkain's dragging behind me. Speaking of my mate, he looks very handsome in his black armor. He came inside me barely over an hour ago and already I hunger for him again. He smiles as I approach him, no doubt thinking the same thing, and helps me onto the dais.

Behind him I see something that makes me gasp.

A second throne, identical to his. I am speechless, so I do something that requires no words. I plant a kiss on his lips as the crowd below cheers for us. I see the love I have for him shining back at me. This double throne is a sign that I am a permanent fixture here. That we will rule Myrkorvin together.

A new age for our people starts today, and I cannot wait for it.

A few words from a priest are recited and before long, Arkain is slipping a pointed black crown on my head. Identical to the one he wears. Not exactly my style but I guess I can work with it.

We turn and face the crowd as another cheer goes up. Raising our clasped hands, streamers and dried flowers are tossed into the air. My family is smiling. Even Garren. It truly is a miracle.

Arkain leads me from the dais and we make our way through the throne room and out the side door. We walk along the stone path as the roar of the crowd inside quiets down. I am not even aware of where we are going until I find myself at the base of the glowing willow tree.

"What are we doing out here?"

"I thought for our first time together now that you are officially queen, we could spend it where I first fell in love with you."

I'm speechless, so I kiss him instead of saying anything. He deepens it, pushing my front against him. The hunger I always feel for him comes roaring to the surface and I bite down on his lip. He chuckles, grinding his cock against me.

"Any requests on how I take you this first time, my queen?"

"Only one," I say and he raises an eyebrow.

"Let's leave the crowns on," I say before pulling him down on top of me.

EPILOGUE

ARKAIN
1 YEAR LATER

"Arkain"—Elvie moans, her fingers digging into my scalp—"you're wrinkling my gown!"

Despite her protest, her heels push into my back, urging me to eat her cunt faster. Scraping my fangs over her clit and stretching her with two of my fingers has her clawing at the bed sheets. Her pink gown is in tatters around her waist.

"Do you want me to stop?" I ask, removing my mouth from her sweet flesh. She cries and squeezes my head with her thighs, urging me to get back to my task. Running a claw through her wetness, I chuckle against her and hear her let out a soft sigh. "I didn't think so."

My mate is close. So close in fact that a few more twists and…she lets out a satisfied moan as my claws tickle that secret spot inside of her. She is panting and shaking, her floral scent becoming richer, and then she is exploding on my tongue and I eagerly drink it all down.

She is sweeter than any wine.

Pulling my fingers from her tight cunt, I flip her over on all fours and slam into her. Her moan catches in her throat and she reaches up to grasp the wooden headboard until her knuckles turn white. I run my claws over the curve of her ass and slowly dip a finger through that tight ring of muscle. She hisses before reaching back to swat at me.

"Not there," she moans. "It's still sore from you fucking it last night."

"Are you sure?" I ask, circling it with a claw and being rewarded by her cunt clamping around my cock. "Seems to me like your body is saying

181

something different."

"What is your new found obsession with my ass?" she asks, and I laugh, spanking one pale globe with my hand and watching color bloom. Burying her face in the sheets, she moans again.

"I'm obsessed with every part of you, my wife."

"Can you hurry up and come? We're already late."

"They should expect that by now. Besides…" I reach down and pull her up so I'm still on my knees behind her, but her back is pressed to my front. "If you want to make me come fast you know what to say."

I like the sensitive pointed tip of her ear and she moans, tilting her head back just enough to meet my eyes.

"I love you."

That unleashes the beast inside of me. I pound into her over and over. Her breasts bouncing and the sound of flesh slapping together is my favorite song. No matter how many times I hear it, I want to hear it again and again. One touch of her clit with my claw and she's done for.

Her inner muscles squeeze me so tight as I spill my seed inside of her. This is perfection and I would stay buried inside her all day, but my wife, the kind soul that she is, has other plans for us.

Pulling out of her, I help secure her dress back into place and fix the loose hairs that have escaped around her face. Then without even batting an eye, we make the journey from our room to the throne room. It is the one day a month where we hear from our subjects directly.

After Elvie decreed the bridge to be open to all who wished to use it, that inspired her to have more transparency with our people. So anyone, from human to noble, can come talk to us freely.

As we make our way through the throne room, it's hard to remember a time where dark and light elves did not both inhabit this space. Elvie and I are far from the only dark and light elf mates. What that means for our kind, I do not know.

But that deep primal part of me cannot wait to find out. Elvie has been talking about coming off her contraceptive tea. It's hard enough to conceive as elves anyway and if we were to be blessed with a child, it would grow up wanting for nothing.

The thought of Elvie round with my child...my cock grows hard and she raises a brow at me. I kiss her forehead and motion to the guard for us to hear the first subject.

Elvie and I are both shocked when the pink-haired Kaethe steps in front of us.

"Your Majesties," she says and drops into a curtsy.

"Kaethe? You wish to ask us for something?"

"I do, my queen. I would ask that you and the king allow me to travel to the Brokenbone Mountains," she says calmly. A few shocked gasps ring out behind her. They are right to be shocked. A human wanting to go into the heart of orc territory. Not even elves are brave enough to do that. She pushes on, "I've heard whispers of a human living amongst them. A man, taken in as a child. It could just be a rumor but I believe it could be—"

"Your brother," Elvie finishes for her. "Kae, that's a tremendous risk to take for something we have no reliable information on."

"It's been whispered about for years, Kaethe." My voice must be too sharp as my wife cuts me a disapproving look. I press on, in what I hope is a gentler tone. "We've never had any indication that is the case. Besides, you more than anyone know the rules. Humans are forbidden from entering the orc lands. And by the same token, orcs are forbidden from stealing humans as per the treaty we signed at the end of the war. If there is a human there, it is highly doubtful he is there by choice."

"I understand the risks, Your Majesties. But I have lived for years wondering if it is him. Wondering if he's just been waiting there all this time for me to find him." She straightens her spine and lifts her delicate chin. "With peace between our two kingdoms, I could go there as your royal...envoy. To make sure everything is being adhered to. If nothing else, it would allow me to continue my work on creating an antidote for the orc's teeth poison."

"And what will you do if you find him, Kae? If your brother has been held there all this time?"

Kaethe pauses and then levels me with a stare that would frighten most males.

"Under the treaty signed that ended the Orc Wars, humans found

183

on orc lands that can be proven to be there against their will can claim asylum in Myrkorvin." Gods spare me, I choke on a laugh and shake my head. I knew that clause would come back to bite me. That's what I get for trying to impress my nobles as a new king.

Elvie glances over at me with her brows raised.

"Kaethe," I say, making one last effort to put her off of this mission, "the orc mountains are dangerous. It is going to be winter soon, the elements out there are unforgiving." I pause. "Not to mention that the orcs will most likely view you as a meal."

Elvie elbows me and shakes her head. What? It's the truth.

"I know the risks, Your Majesties. But this is really important to me. I wouldn't ask for this if it wasn't."

I look over at Elvie who has a pleading look on face, she mouths the word please and I groan. Who am I to deny my queen?

"Fine. You are permitted to go. But a warning to you, if things go awry out there, I cannot promise to send anyone to rescue you. You will be very much on your own."

"Thank you, your majesties. I understand the risks."

"We will miss you fiercely, my friend," Elvie says with a warm smile, gliding down the steps of the dais to embrace the human. They hug for a moment, Elvie's chin resting atop Kathe's magenta head. The two disentangle, both with unshed tears in their eyes as Kaethe bows and retreats out of the hall. I reach over to grasp Elvie's hand and bring it to my lips.

"If you asked me for the sun I would find a way to give it to you. I can deny you nothing, my love."

"I'm glad you said that because there is something I've been wanting for a while now," she says, biting her lip.

"And what's that?"

"A baby," She says softly, a small smile playing on her lips. I stop breathing for a moment even as joy bursts through me. That's how every day with Elvie has been. Pure joy, love, and happiness. And now she's ready to start us on a new adventure.

One that I am more than happy to start right now.

"You're sure?" I ask.

"Quite sure," she says and I pull her to her feet before tossing her over my shoulders.

"My people, I regret to inform you that the queen requires me to attend to an urgent matter. We will be postponing these hearings until tomorrow." I pause considering that. "Actually until next week. I thank you for your understanding."

Grumbling and confused shouts follow us from the throne room but the sweet sound of Elvie's laugh drowns them all out. Opening the door to our room I lay her down on the bed, her glowing face smiling up at me.

"Really? You just had me less than an hour ago?" She smiles up at me and I know my answering smile is just as radiant. How could it not me? The gods gave me the most perfect female as my wife, my queen, my love…and soon to be the mother to my children.

"And I need to have you again. And again after that. So many times that you won't remember the last time you moved and my seed did not leak from you." I strip out of my ridiculous court attire and watch Elvie rake appreciative eyes down my body. My female needs me again. She'll need me forever, just like I will need her. Unending, just like our love.

"I love you," I say, ripping the front of her gown until her breasts spill out.

"I love you too," she says, shimmying the garment off. "Now get me pregnant."

I fall between her soft, spread thighs and get to work doing just that.

THE END

ACKNOWLEDGEMENTS

Firstly, I want to say thank you to the people who helped make this book possible. The map and interior formatting done by Qamber Designs & Media went beyond my wildest dreams. Magdalena Pietrzak (@barnswallow.art) for creating the most beautiful cover I have ever seen, and Haya from Haya Designs putting the finishing touches on it to make it look like an actual cover. I also want to thank my editor from Aquila editing for taking my rough draft and turning it into the version you all are seeing today!

Alright, now onto the sappy stuff and if you think I'm crying while writing this…that's not important. Firstly, a huge shoutout to my parents (I'm serious, I hope you guys never read this book). Mom and Dad, without your unwavering support in me and my pursuit of some unorthodox ventures, I do not know where I would be today. Maybe my hero in this book wouldn't be a monster but who are we to speculate on the 'what-if's of life. I love you both so much.

To my friends, that you for always supporting me even when you really didn't understand what I was doing. There are bits of all of you sprinkled in this book and all of my books to come.

Thank you so much to my online support system. My beta and ARC readers, you all really went above and beyond for me and I cannot thank you enough. For a debut novel to have that much interest shown in it by all of you I am truly grateful for.

To my readers who took a chance on my debut monster romance, thank you. There is so much of this world I want to explore with you and I am eternally grateful that you gave my book a chance.

I feel like saying thank you to TikTok feels very *Black Mirror*-y but it deserves a shoutout in here as well. Without that platform, I wouldn't have found myself. I wouldn't have any of the skills, tools, and encouragement I found on that platform to complete the book you have read today. So thank you, for what you have taught me and for the people I have met because of you. Speaking of which…

Last, but certainly not least, for you Kayla. This was our adventure, as much as it was my own. Without you, truly none of this would've happened. The internet has a way of bringing people together and I'm forever grateful it brought me you. So, thank you for everything.

MEET THE AUTHOR

CHARLOTTE SWAN is twenty-four year old, living in Chicago. When she is not dreaming about being whisked away to a world filled with magic and sexy monsters, she is busy being a freelance social media marketer and full-time smut lover. To hear about her upcoming projects or to connect with her on social media please find her on her website or by scanning the code below.

www.authorcharlotteswan.com

Printed in Great Britain
by Amazon